BESS

As a child in Plymouth Bess Morten used to watch the ships of Francis Drake and John Hawkins setting sail for the New World. She wished that she, too, might journey to those strange lands and refused to listen to people who reminded her that a woman's place was at home, waiting for the men to return from their adventures. She was determined to see the world for herself – especially when she discovered she had a half-brother living among the Cimaroons on the Darien shore.

The quest for Matthew Morten took Bess into a new life and another dream. As the boy Ben Moore, she sailed the Atlantic and rode with the buccaneers. Finally in the land of the Cimaroons she found more than she was seeking.

From this point on, Bess dreamed only of gaining control of her own fortune so that she could finance a colony on the beautiful island of Maravila. The realization of this ambition proved to be even more difficult and dangerous than her Caribbean quest.

Bess's story is a sequel to that of her brother Matthew, which was told in *'Maroon Boy*.

BY THE SAME AUTHOR

Beyond the Dragon Prow
'Maroon Boy

Robert Leeson
BESS

COLLINS *St James's Place* · London

William Collins Sons & Co Ltd
London · Glasgow · Sydney · Auckland
Toronto · Johannesburg

First published 1975
© Robert Leeson 1975
ISBN 0 00 184051 7
Made and printed in Great Britain by
William Collins Sons & Co Ltd Glasgow

Maravila Island, where Bess tried to make her dream come true, does not exist. But dreams have their power. For many years in the seventeenth century Fonceta Island in the Caribbean appeared on maps, and King Charles I granted charters for settlers to go there. Yet there was no Fonceta Island.

And at this same time, in the jungle of South America not far from the Caribbean shore, escaped slaves set up a Cimaroon 'Republic' which lasted nearly a hundred years.

For Christine and Fred

Chapter one

A pikeman on watch below the bastion saw a faint greying in the sky eastwards.

'Night soon over lads,' he called.

The others, whose pikes were stacked by the fort wall, barely turned from the red glow of the brazier. For July the air was cold. The wind gusted in over Plymouth Sound, ripping foam from the waves. The watcher spoke again.

' 'Tis the Sabbath.'

A young man raised his head. 'Aye, but we'll not be in church today.'

Another laughed. 'Thou'rt never in church. I'll wager this is thy first Sunday morn without a thick head.'

'Aye,' said another, 'Harry's sober. Lord, thy wonders cease not.'

' 'Tis not the Lord's doing – 'tis the Spanish Fleet's. His hand shook so last night, it held not the cup.'

The young man was suddenly angry. 'Who says I'm feared of the Spaniards?'

'Only a jest, lad,' said an older man. 'But, no shame, there's plenty afraid.'

'Aye, and some have taken bag and baggage and fled.'

'That's not the Armada they fled, 'twas the plague.'

'They say Lord Howard's lost one man in three before the battle's started. Others were too sick to go on board.'

'If that be so, how can we win?'

' 'Tis all up with old England, if not.'

Young Harry spoke up. ' 'Twas a marvel our ships did clear harbour. The Spaniards sailed but a bow shot from the shore.'

Someone laughed. 'A bow shot, lad. Thou'rt dreaming.'

'Nay, 'tis true. I stood on Staddon Heights and saw them. They were so close I might have spat upon them.'

'And why didst thou not?'

'I'm no fool. The wind did blow from seaward.'

Footsteps from the road above cut short the laughter. The watcher called, 'Who comes?'

'Officer of the watch.'

'Look lively, lads. Take up your pikes. Jacob Morten's officer this night.'

'Morten? I know him not.'

'Why there's hardly a fishing boat that sails to Newfoundland Banks but he has a share in it.'

'And in his time he was a great preacher. Men came from Tavistock and Exeter to hear him.'

'Man of fish, Man of God? What does he know of war?'

'Before thou wert born, lad, he fought the Turk outside Vienna, and he fought the Cornish rebels in '49. Aye and the Queen's men too...'

'Here he comes.'

Three men in dark cloaks appeared. Their leader was tall but bent with age and his hair gleamed white above the snowy lace of the collar. His eyes went rapidly over the small file of men and stopped at Harry.

'Nay, lad. Do thou hold the pike – not the pike hold thee.'

Harry shifted awkwardly.

'Shall we fight this day, Master Morten?' he asked.

'Not on land. Our ships have got to windward of the Dons. Soon you'll hear the cannon. Only captive Spaniards land in Plymouth today. Take your ease, lads.'

The watch clustered round the brazier again. Morten's fellow officers said 'Good morrow,' and left. But Morten said, 'I'll stay here. The ferryman waits across the Cattewater, there, to bring me news of my wife.'

'True. God send her well – '

Morten walked stiffly to the water's edge and sat on a low wall, looking into the slowly lightening sky.

'What's with his wife? Is she sick?' asked Harry.

The others laughed.

'Nay, she's with child. He sent her over to be with her kin at Ancombe Ferrers.'

'I trow 'tis his last chance. When a man's so old and rich, he longs for an heir.'

'Has he no other children?'

'He had one. Reuben, a godly lad but sickly. He died two years since.'

'I heard tell of another son . . .'

'Nay . . . he had no other . . .'

'I'll stake my credit he'd another son . .'

'Thy credit counts for nought. And quiet now or he'll hear.'

Slowly, the moments passed. Then someone pointed across the water.

'There comes the ferryman.'

As the boat drew nearer, the ferryman pulling it on with sure, strong strokes, Morten began to pace at the water's edge. Finally he could wait no longer. Cupping hand to mouth he shouted :

'What news?'

The boatman paused in his rowing and turned his head. His voice came faintly over the water.

"Tis a maid.'

'A maid, eh, Mr Morten?' called the pikemen.

'Aye, praise God for His blessing,' the old man murmured.

'And what shall she be called?'

A gleam came into Morten's eyes. He turned and raised his hand.

'Call her? Why Elizabeth, after our Queen – Bess.'

Two miles away over the water, in a farmhouse, at Ancombe

Ferrers, the midwife handed over the newborn girl to a nurse.

'See how thick the hair is on the head – how black. And she's red like a cherry,' said the woman.

The midwife said nothing. The birth had been hard, too hard for the mother, who now lay still on the bed, eyes closed for the last time.

Chapter two

Before Bess Morten was a week old, the Spanish Armada was scattered or sunk, burnt to the waterline by Drake's fire ships.

That winter no ship came across the Channel to buy fish in Plymouth. News was that King Philip of Spain planned another invasion. Jacob Morten's ships dumped their catch and the old man sat in his counting house in Stillman Street near Sutton Pool going through his ledgers. Maybe he should sell ships and buy land.

When Bess learned to walk, tottering across the floor of the Broad Chamber, Plymouth swarmed with soldiers fresh from the wars in Holland, now shipping for raids on Lisbon and the Azores. But fever and the flux struck down the fleet before it could sail. Men with long purses took their families and fled the port. Morten scorned to do this, but he looked at the bright-eyed, black-haired girl as she played in the gallery over the courtyard and he wondered what to do for her safety.

When Bess was three she sat before her father on a horse, while they rode amid a crowd of merchants in black and brown, gentlemen and their ladies dressed in red and blue, out to the open fields that led up to the moors. She saw the flash of gold from the gorse, smelled the honeyed scent of the heather, saw a buzzard circle in the blue sky.

A great cheer rose as water, drawn from the Meavy's stream, flowed into a freshly dug course and trickled down towards the city. Canny Jacob Morten counted up the cost of piping needed to connect his home to the new water supply

– provided thanks to Sir Francis Drake's project. Morten counted the cost and decided to wait. Meanwhile the servants could go to the pump.

Fleets sailed and docked. New warehouses grew along the harbour edge. When Bess was six she saw a prize ship brought into port, and sailors' children played with trinkets and ribbons by the roadside, while hucksters swarmed into town to buy looted Spanish pearls.

When Bess was seven she would slip out from the side door of her father's warehouse and run down to the harbour. At the jetty on South Side, Will Curnock, her father's most skilful skipper waited on the deck of his fishing vessel. He would pull off his woollen cap and say:

'Now, Mistress Morten. What shall it be – across the Sound to Cawsand Bay and back for supper?'

And Tom, his stocky, curly-haired ten-year-old son would chuckle as Bess stamped her foot and cried:

'Nay, to the world's end.'

She sat in the prow with Tom and watched as Drake and Hawkins set sail on another voyage Westward to skin the Spaniards of their golden fleece yet again. The ships came home again leaving Hawkins, Drake and many of their crews beneath the waves off faraway Porto Bello. Seamen roamed the streets with licence to beg and one day Bess saw a dead man lying by the roadside. His skin was black and his open eyes gleamed white at the sky. She ran home in fear.

That summer Jacob Morten sent her, with young Tom, to stay on the farm he had bought, near the moors. John Coppin, his tenant, and his wife Mabel made Bess welcome. And for playmate she had Judith, their daughter, two years older. Together with Tom they roamed and climbed and laughed and quarrelled and fought. Judith gave in soon, acknowledging Tom's sturdy strength. But Bess would fight to the last.

A pony was brought from the moor for her to ride. She clung tight-fisted to its mane and beat its back with her bare heels as the half-tamed creature shied.

'Run,' shouted old Coppin to one of his men. 'Catch him. The devil's in the beast.'

'Nay,' laughed the man, 'the devil's in the rider.'

Each autumn Bess, her hair as wild as the ponies she rode, was brought back into town. Tom Curnock was sent to work with his father, mending nets, pitching and caulking the boats, repairing sails. Bess would run down to the port and old Ben would greet her . . . 'Now, Mistress Morten . . .'

One evening when she was ten, her father's partners, Simon Rishworth and Mordecai Trant and their wives came to dine. After Bess had said her good nights and was led from the Broad Chamber to her bedroom, gaunt Alice Trant turned and remarked :

' 'Twill take many years to make a lady of that wild creature.'

Jacob grunted. But he had heard. Next month, Margaret Bray, a quiet spinster in a grey gown, moved into the house to teach Bess her lessons. She learned quickly. She would climb on a stool in his counting house and running a finger down the pages, call out . . . 'Mr Hollis . . . debtor . . . Mr Hawkes . . . desperate debtor . . .'

She learned quickly – those things she wished to learn. When Margaret instructed her in the ways of behaviour and management of the household, Bess would turn and gaze from the Broad Chamber window at the masts and rigging that showed above the roofs. But evening drew on and candles were lit and Margaret took from the great oak chest by the window books of discovery and voyages, tales of far ports and cities. Then Bess would crouch in the broad window ledge, head in hands and listen, while Margaret read.

'I would I might journey to those lands,' said Bess.

'Women go not abroad. That men must do.'

'And what shall women?'

'Why, Bess, see that all's well and wait till men shall return.'

'Nay, I'll wait for no man,' said Bess. She leapt down from the window ledge. 'Say, what other books are there, we have

not read? What's that small one beneath Mr Hakluyt's book?'
' 'Tis nought.'
Bess reached in and plucked the volume out.
'Why, 'tis verse.' She paced the room and held the book up.
'When first mine eye did light upon . . .' Margaret flushed. 'Nay Mistress Elizabeth. Thy father will be wroth.'
Bess thrust the book back into the chest and rummaged further and drew out another volume. 'Bartoleme las Casas. Why 'tis in a foreign tongue.'
'Spanish.'
Bess turned the pages.
' 'Tis writ here . . . Matthew Morten, his book.'
Margaret shook her head. 'I know not who that might be. Yet, stay. Didst thou not have a brother who died young?'
'That's so,' said Bess. 'Some of these books are his. But his name was Reuben and he died 'ere I was born.'
Margaret nodded. 'Reuben, son of Jacob. Your father loved him well.'
Margaret took the book from Bess's hand and closed the chest. 'Here comes Dame Anna to see you to your bed,' she said as the old housekeeper came with hand-shielded candle to the door.
'Dame Anna must know for sure,' said Besss.
'What must I know?' said the old dame, surprised.
'Why, who was Matthew that could read Spanish?'
'Nay, I know no Matthew,' she answered sharply.
'Thou liest,' said Bess, beneath her breath.
Next day she sought out her father in the counting house. He turned from his ledgers and peered at her. She knew that now he could barely see her across the room.
'Who is Matthew, Father?'
A spark flared in his eye, then was gone.
'Matthew,' he said dully. 'I know no Matthew.'
'A Morten, one of our family.'
His voice raised. 'I know no Matthew.'

Chapter three

The summer Bess was thirteen, she went to the farm without Tom for the first time. Tom, now strong and broad-chested, though no taller than Bess, sailed with his father to the cod banks. Her playmate had gone and she knew that when he returned he would not come back to play on the moorland slopes.

At Coppins', Judith was poor company. She was busy around the house and yard, or bent over the kitchen range. When no other task called, she sat in the narrow hall of the farmhouse at her spinning wheel, talking to her mother and sisters, or more often gazing out into the distance.

Even when her mother set her free from work to go with Bess, Judith said little but answered only when Bess pressed her and then with a 'yea' or 'nay'.

'What ails thee, Judith?'

'Nought.'

Bess asked Goodie Coppin.

'Say, have I offended Judith? She will not walk and talk with me.'

The goodwife smiled and folded her arms.

'Now what ails Judith? 'Tis the oldest sickness in the world.'

'I understand thee not.'

'Why Mistress 'Lisbeth, Judith will not be well until the fishing fleet's home again.'

'Tom!' cried Bess.

'Aye, Tom.'
'But Judith is too...'
'Judith is fourteen.'
'But I will soon be fourteen.'
'Then, haply wilt thou think on these things too.'
'Not I. Why should I mope and sulk and sit in corners while the seasons pass me by?'
'And what else wilt thou?'
'I'll over the moors or over the sea – to New Spain or Virginia,' said Bess suddenly.

The old woman smiled.
'A strange fancy.'

One day Bess went into the yard to see Crispin, one of the Coppin boys, lead in a fine chestnut horse, a lively two-year-old, ready saddled.

'Whence came this beauty?' she asked.

He shook his head shyly, but held the horse's head and gestured to her to mount.

' 'Tis a gift from thy father,' said old Coppin standing in the farmhouse door. 'Now Crispin, do thou lead him for a while till Mistress Morten has the feel of him.'

Down the road Bess coaxed the chestnut into a gentle trot while Crispin ran beside her. As they rode into the village, she saw two young men on horseback. They were gentlemen's sons, well mounted and elegantly dressed: one slim and neat, pale with yellow hair and, it seemed to Bess, a kindly face; the other, a head taller and broadly built, had a reckless face, beneath red-brown hair.

Bess asked: 'Who are those gentlemen?'

Crispin replied.

'One's Master Hugh Dauncey. His father's manor is beyond the village. 'Tis said they're papists.'

'Which one is he?'

'The little one.'

'And the other?'

'Ah, he's a cousin. I've heard say he's a Ferrers from Plymstock way.'

Bess heard hooves on the road. Yelling and laughing, the two young men swept past her. The chestnut jerked in her hands and on impulse she set off in pursuit of the two who were already mounting the hill ahead.

Crispin called out, and too late Bess realized her mistake. Riding side-saddle and hampered by her long skirt she could not control the horse at that speed. In a second she was rolling over foolishly on the grass, while the excited horse capered across the track. Crispin ran up anxiously.

'Go get the horse. I'll see to myself,' she called.

Relieved, Crispin hid a grin and obeyed, leaving Bess to follow. She rode back to the farm more slowly, biting her lips with vexation. She felt sure that Dauncey and Ferrers had planned to outface her and had seen her downfall.

That night as she made ready for bed, she called Judith.

'Canst thou beg some clothes of thy brother for me?'

Judith's eyes grew round in the faint glow of the rushlight.

'What manner of clothes?'

'A shirt, breeches.'

Judith laughed.

' 'Tis a jest.'

'Nay. I'll pay him for them. He shall have a crown.'

'For that he'll give thee boots and hose. But, say what manner of sport do you plan?'

'No sport. I'll ride that chestnut at a gallop without being cast off. No more than that.'

'Wilt ride as a man?'

'I'll ride as a maid, but astride the beast. Say thou'lt do't Judith, and I'll do thee a service.'

'What manner of service . . . ?'

'This autumn, when I go back to Plymouth, wilt thou come with me, as my maid? That's for the form. I mean to keep me company. Margaret Bray is a good gentle lady, but our moods do not match. Besides, the air in Sutton Pool will suit thee well.'

Judith sprang from the stool and kissed Bess fiercely.

'Art a true, kind good Bess.'

'Kind and good am I not. But true, I hope. Now, maid, prithee comb out my hair. And when that's done . . .'

'Aye?'

'Then I'll comb out thine.'

Next day, in shirt, breeches and boots, her hair bound up, Bess mounted the chestnut behind the barn and rode him trot, canter, gallop over the meadows and tracks, the wind in her face and wild excitement in her heart. But if she secretly expected to meet Dauncey and his cousin she was disappointed.

Autumn came and she returned to Plymouth with Judith. She found her father more irritable, as he struggled with failing eyesight. One afternoon while he dozed in his great chair, Bess went into the counting house and with the aid of the clerk, Ned Wallis, examined the accounts. Errors were creeping in which Wallis had not spoken of, fearing Jacob's temper too much. As soon as the old man woke, Bess told him what she had found. For a moment her father blustered but soon agreed that his eyes might fool him now and then.

From then on, Bess worked each morning in the counting house and warehouse or went to the fish quay talking with merchants and seamen. Most had known her from childhood and had a healthy respect for her temper. Those who had not soon learned.

'Ah, here comes Mistress Morten,' said one portly merchant. 'Happy the man who shall have her for his bride. He'll live in wealth and idleness all his days.'

'Ah,' retorted Bess. 'Happy the man that knows how to guard his tongue. He shall live free of offence all his days.'

His friends laughed and she went on her way to a chorus of 'Good morrows.'

One evening Jacob's partners and their wives came to dine and to her surprise, Jacob asked Bess to join them.

'Thou shalt be the lady of the house now and order the meal,' he said.

Bess wrinkled her nose.

'Nay, let rather Dame Anna do it. Why should I take her place?'

Jacob frowned.

'Do as I say.'

That night Bess, in a new long-sleeved gown with a stiff bodice that made her ribs ache, and her hair bound in a coif, sat uncomfortably at table, while the amiable Rishworth and his wife Rachel paid her compliments and even the lantern-jawed Trant and his gaunt wife Alice eyed her with new respect.

But as the meal ended, Bess understood by nods and eyebrow twitches from her father that she was now expected to rise and lead the ladies into the parlour while the men discussed their business. For an hour she sat in a high-backed chair listening to town gossip, recipes for preserves, remedies for the croup and complaints at prices in the market, and parrying hints and questions of marriage prospects.

Then as the Rishworths and Trants left, she spoke to her father.

'Father. It is not just that I should labour at thy accounts in the morning and be banished from thy councils in the evening.'

Jacob's eyes were wrathful.

' 'Tis thy duty and thy place. So will it be when thou art wed. As thou hast learnt to read and write, so shalt thou learn the graces of a good family.'

'But . . .' she began.

His face darkened. 'Art as headstrong even as . . .' he broke off as if he had said too much and stumped away.

Angrily Bess called for Judith, but got no answer. She

walked out on to the gallery and called into the courtyard. Again, no answer. But from below came the sound of cheerful voices. She ran down the stairs, across the courtyard and into the kitchen. As she threw open the door, the noise stopped.

The servants round the great scrubbed table looked up from their beer pots. The cook, a leg of chicken in her podgy fingers, stopped with it half-way to her mouth. By the fire sat Tom Curnock, his face ruddy from the flames, his arm around Judith. In the other corner sat Margaret Bray, a small thimble glass in her hand, her eyes cast down.

Bess's anger vanished.

'Nay, people. 'Tis but Bess.'

Tom leapt to his feet and drew out a stool. He looked at Bess as she stood in the doorway, tall and slender, her face darkly flushed above the white frill at her throat.

'Nay, be seated, Mistress Morten,' he said.

'Hast been on a long voyage, Tom Curnock. I was Bess before.'

He grinned and placed the stool before her. She sat down.

'Now, what was it you spoke of – or is it secret?'

There was silence. Then Judith said, 'We did speak of men and maids . . .'

'Aye. What's new in that?'

'We did debate,' said Tom, 'which of the two were better.'

'Nay,' said Ned Wallis, the clerk, who sat near Margaret Bray. 'There was no debate. 'Tis a foregone conclusion.'

'What?' cried the cook.

'Since Eve was made of Adam's rib, 'tis clear, who's the better.'

'Ha,' retorted the cook, 'and of what was Adam made? What doth the Book say? "the dust of the ground".'

'And did not Eve lead Adam into sin?'

'Aye she offered him to eat and like a cormorant he took it.'

'And what else doth the Book say? Man shall love, but woman shall obey?'

'How can she obey if he love not?'

'Or he love if she obey not?'

When the laughter died down, Margaret Bray spoke up quietly. 'My mother did say, if the oxen be not equal in the yoke, the plough will not run straight.'

'I know nought of oxen,' gasped the cook, wiping her eyes. 'But this I do know. There are as many good men in Devon as there are white bulls.'

'And as many good women,' shouted Wallis, 'as black swans.'

'But where would men be without women to help them?' called Judith from the fireplace.

'Aye,' chuckled Tom, 'women helpeth man – to consume all he earns,' and he held up his arm to ward off a blow from his sweetheart.

'And consume she doth, in fads and fancies,' said Wallis, looking round. 'Buy her a dress and straightaway she must parade before her neighbours. Buy it not and she grumbles.'

'Why so grudging?' flashed Judith. 'She hath the management of the home, and a full belly maketh a glad heart.'

'Well, let the woman rule the roast, if the man can rule the roost.'

Bess could keep quiet no longer.

'Why should he rule the roost?'

Wallis put on a solemn face. 'Woman is by nature like the moon. She waxeth and waneth and is ever fickle. Man is like the sun, fiery and constant.'

The cook shouted: 'And the farther off the moon is from the sun, the brighter she shines. And the farther woman is from man, the merrier she is.'

Tom waved his ale pot, and burst into song.

> 'They rune, they range,
> Their minds do change,
> They make their friend their foe,
> As lovers true,
> Each day a new...'

And all joined in the chorus:

> '*But I must not say so.*'

Ned Wallis, in a high-pitched, cracked voice, took up the song:

> '*Give this, give that
> All things they lack
> And all you may bestow,
> Once out of sight,
> Farewell, good night.*'

> '*But I must not say so.*'

Amid laughter and hand-clapping the kitchen door opened. Dame Alice stood there.
   'Abate your noise, good people. Master Morten calls us all to the Broad Chamber for evening prayers.'

Chapter four

That winter, Jacob Morten was eighty. A will like iron kept him at his business and his inner vanity kept him finely, if soberly dressed, at all times of day. He could no longer read, neither his ledgers nor his Bible.

He grew more demanding on Bess and each day half her time was spent in the counting house, while one hour at sunset was spent in the Broad Chamber reading to him. Yet in other things she was free. The management of the house, and the money that went with it, was given over to her. For the first time she chose her own clothes, with Judith an eager helper and adviser and Margaret Bray in the background with her quiet words of warning.

'Heigh-ho,' said Bess to Judith, as she stood one day in the cold light of a winter afternoon which filtered into her bedroom. 'I have thee to tell me what I may and Margaret to tell me what I may not. But it is passing strange. Last year my dresses were too short for my arms, now they pinch me in the waist.'

Judith put her hands to Bess's hips and pressed gently.

'Thy body doth alter, as it must, if thou wilt be woman and bear children.'

'How shall I know when that will be?'

Judith shrugged. 'Thou wilt know it when it comes. When thy bosom swells, grows tender. A heaviness within thee top to toe. An ache, a pain, and later a lightness,' she paused 'as though the tide did ebb and flow throughout thee.'

25

'Ha. Wallis was right. So like the moon we are. And is it always so?'

'Aye, each month, 'an we like it or not.'

Bess paced the room.

'That's not to my liking – like it or not.'

Judith stared at her. 'But how shall woman else? If she's to bear children?'

'Say, Judith,' Bess's voice lowered, 'when a woman is with child, there's hurt and harm. My mother did die when I was born.'

'Woman and man must die, Bess. And children must be born. Who's to say nay. But hurt? Hast thou not marked, at Coppins' how the cattle bring forth the young, some quietly, some with noise and complaint.'

'Aye, but the beasts do not choose nor understand. We are not beasts.'

'Choose?' asked Judith, her eyes clouded. 'It is a woman's way, it is the way of love.'

'But, how's one to know by looking at a man, if that be love?'

Judith, her eyes still far away, smiled broadly. She sang:

>'How shall I my true love know?
>By his woollen fisher's cap,
>By his merry . . .'

'Have done, Judith. That's a song too saucy for younger ears . . .'

Margaret Bray stood in the doorway.

Judith frowned. 'What dost thou know of these things – that no man has looked on?'

Margaret's voice was quiet. 'When I was of thine age, Judith, two men came courting me. Him that I loved did not suit my father. Him that my father chose did not suit me. And while we disputed, both departed. May thou have better fortune.'

Judith walked from the room. Bess stretched out her hand.
'Be not wroth, Margaret. Judith is young.'
Margaret smiled: 'Not half so old as thee, Bess. Thy father bids thee come . . .'
'And bring the Book . . . ?' said Bess.
Margaret nodded. She took Bess's hand. 'Oh, Bess, be not too proud.'
Bess found her father in the great oak chair before the window of the Broad Chamber. She sat down in the window seat and took up the Bible to read. Her father's sharp-featured face was soft, the eyes were closed, but she knew he listened. As the chapter ended he murmured.
'Send for wine. Simon Rishworth and Mordecai Trant will be here soon. And do thou stay with us. I'll need thee to prompt me if I forget ought.'
Bess went herself to the cellar and brought up the wine. When she came back her father's partners were in their places. Rishworth bobbed and smiled. Trant nodded and they went on with the conversation. Trant was speaking.
'We're pressed from two sides, Jacob. On the Banks the Dutch and French steal the fish from before our noses. And London merchants steal the trade from behind our backs.'
'True,' added Rishworth, 'they build their cellars outside the town and if that's not enough, they escape taxes. These past two years our gain has fallen off.'
' 'Tis a pin-prick,' said Jacob.
' 'Tis no affair of mine,' said Trant, 'but thou hast put thine own free money these past three years into sheep pasture, not keels and rigging.'
'And thou'rt free to do likewise. What we debate is how we venture that stock we hold together. And forget not the half is mine.'
'Aye, that we cannot forget,' said Rishworth, 'but I'll tell thee Jacob, I'm for a change. We own ten vessels whole and shares in ten more. Let's put two of our bigger craft in next year's venture to the Spanish Islands.'

'Privateering?' said Jacob.

The others nodded. Jacob shook his head vigorously.

'Why not go down to Sutton Pool and cast your gold into the mud. 'Twill take less labour.'

'Others have grown richer than we and faster.'

'And others have beggared themselves.' Jacob heaved himself up. 'While fools in Devon chase Spanish gold and catch only fever and the flux, cunning men in London ship spices and saltpetre and wax fat at home.'

'Now Jacob, we meant but a small venture.'

Jacob snorted: 'A small hole in thy pocket will let fall thy coin. The wise man sees when evil cometh and makes good his defence.'

He drained his glass.

'Have ye not marked how for all the gold lace on ladies' collars, the port is going down? One year it swarms with soldiers, next year it's empty. Men put their gold in trade and fools believe in war.'

His voice lowered.

'I hear that the Queen – God defend her – has not long to live. And do you believe this war with Spain, which has beggared our land, will go on? Nay, there'll be peace. And he who seizes Spanish ships will be hanged in London if he's not burnt in Seville. Nay, my gold's in fish, in land, in corn, in sheep, and there it stays.'

The others were silent.

'But we must talk of other things. Like our monarch I grow old.'

Rishworth and Trant shook their heads.

'Pah,' said Jacob. 'I'll not last another winter, and what's more it's full twelve months since I drew my own balance in the counting house.'

'Aye, God be praised, you've had young Bess to do your figures. A nimble mind,' said Rishworth.

'True,' said Jacob. 'But, it's not in my mind she should fill her days with my affairs. She'll have other things to do.'

Bess stiffened in her chair.

'Aye,' said Trant, 'no doubt there'll be plenty of young men after her fortune. Rest assured though, we shall see to her best interest.'

'Aye,' replied Jacob ironically, 'I know thou'lt see to my fortune and hers as if 'twere thine own.'

Rishworth chuckled and Trant scowled. Jacob went on.

'Ned Wallis is a faithful dog, but he's no longer so young. It is in my mind to put in a new man.'

'Who?'

'I've a letter from a brother of our faith in Yorkshire. He recommends Samuel Fletcher, weaver, self-taught preacher and godly man, lecturer in the parishes. The Bishop there doth frown on him, and denies him a licence to preach, so Fletcher must go.'

'I see the drift,' said Trant. 'He'll do thy accounts and preach the word.'

'Have a care,' said Rishworth, 'that he makes a fair balance 'twixt God's business and thine.'

'Never fear. He has a son, a learned lad, Martin by name, who'll supply any lack.'

'Is it thy meaning I should leave thy affairs alone, Father?' said Bess.

'Nay, but I'll have thee less in the counting house and more in the Broad Chamber and parlour, when folk do call. And I'll have thee even less around the harbour. 'Tis not fitting.'

Bess made as if to speak, but he raised a hand to silence her.

'I would you should rule yourself, rather than be ruled by me. That time has gone.'

Spring came, and the breeze that blew from the moor with its promise of flowers, heather and spring turf, served to sharpen Bess's restlessness. Judith and Tom had got the consent of their parents to marry in two years' time. Will Curnock knew his last Newfoundland voyage was coming and Tom would be master of the ship before he was twenty. So Judith was busy about her own concerns and she could neither share nor understand Bess's feelings.

In June they went to the farm, and Bess dressed for riding in the clothes she secretly borrowed from Crispin. Judith looked at her round-eyed.

'That will not do. Thy bosom begins to betray thee. Here, take this kerchief, bind it round about. Now put on the shirt. Then pin up thy hair under this cap. Nay, 'twill not go.'

'Then cut it and quickly.'

Judith stared.

'Get me a glass and I'll cut it myself.'

The black curly hair was shorn and tucked under the cap and so Bess set out on her ride.

'Thou'rt a handsome groom,' mocked Judith.

'If not a bride,' retorted Bess.

One day as she rode, head down along the road that skirted the moors, she saw Dauncey and Ferrers mounted and blocking her way.

'Give way,' she called, but they did not move. In time she turned the horse's head and swerved past them, catching a glance of Ferrers's insolent face and the hair that gleamed in the sun like her mount's hide. She rode back to the farm in silent rage. When Judith heard she grinned and remarked shrewdly, 'Think Bess. What gentleman would draw aside to let a stable lad go by?'

Bess's face cleared and she laughed in her turn.

Back in Plymouth she found the new arrivals in their place. Samuel Fletcher, a lanky, grey-haired man with a pleasant face and work-worn hands, and Martin his son, pallid and dark-eyed with curling eyelashes. That evening Fletcher spoke and prayed before Jacob and his partners. He took the text 'That which the Lord hath not planted shall be utterly rooted out.'

Bess was astonished to see how now and then a frown would flit across the face of Martin Fletcher and the lad would shake his head as if he disagreed with his father's words. Suddenly Martin saw Bess's eyes on him, blushed red and bent his head.

Each week now, Bess had to entertain her father's guests, merchants from the town or sometimes from Exeter, or now and then officials from the county, or even the Member for the Borough who spoke of disagreements in the House of Commons in London. Then there were local families, parents with their awkward sons, dressed up in new doublets and large flopping white collars. And all, Bess knew, watched her as they ate and talked. As the evenings went by in a train of chatter and awkward pauses, one picture came into her mind again and again. It was of the fair she had ridden to with John Coppin and Crispin, and the sheep and heifers walking in a dusty circle while men thronged around and pointed, counted, argued.

Sometimes the picture angered her. Sometimes it amused her in a twisted way. Sometimes it inspired her at table to make gentle mockery of some young man, ill at ease and hot in his new clothes.

One evening at table, she saw Martin's eyes on her. On his face was the same frown she had seen during the sermon her father preached. To her astonishment he shook his head at her, slightly but distinctly. Piqued she meant to seize the chance to make him explain. But it was not easy to find him alone. Weeks passed and then something happened to drive it from her mind.

She sat one afternoon with Rachel Rishworth, Alice Trant and other ladies, talking of how to spend the fund set up to care for orphans of the fishing fleet.

Mistress Trant spoke of two families that sought help. 'In truth, these children are not orphans. Their fathers live. They are captive on the Barbary Coast.'

Mrs Rishworth shivered. 'Nay, to be taken by the rovers out of Algiers or Sallee, that is to be as dead. May we not aid them?'

'How were these men taken?' asked Bess.

'Why, Mistress Morten,' said a skipper's wife. 'The Sallee Rovers do sail in the Channel these days and snatch our men away.'

'And are there no men-of-war to hinder them?' said Bess.

'Those vessels that go not a-privateering rot in port for lack of care.'

'We've fallen low, then, if the Turk can scour our own waters.'

The others nodded.

'But at least we may aid the children...'

'There are many...' warned Alice Trant.

Bess rounded on her. 'If ye do it unto the least of one of these my children,' she flashed.

Mrs Trant bowed her head. 'Be it so. But a time may come when there are too many mouths to feed.'

As Bess said farewell at the gate of the courtyard, the oldest wife held back.

'Well-spoken, Mistress. There's fire in thee. Why, when thou didst cite the Book, I was put in mind of thy brother.'

'What, of Reuben?'

The old head shook vigorously.

'Nay, of Matthew . . . thy half-brother. Didst not know? Thy father had wife and child before thy mother. Good day, Mistress Morten.'

Chapter five

Bess went back into the house, deep in thought. One mystery that had clouded a corner of her mind since she was a child was made clearer. There was a Matthew Morten, and he was her brother.

But why would no one speak of this Matthew? Why did her father deny him so stubbornly? Why had her father lied to her? She entered the Broad Chamber as the sun was setting. One wall was speckled with yellow diamond shapes of light as the last rays of the sun shone through the window. Her father dozed in his chair, mouth open, cheeks slack. What manner of man was this Matthew? Man he must be, though how old she could not say. If her godly father disowned him, what was his sin? And if people said that she was like him, what was her sin? Suddenly she heard Margaret's voice in her mind 'Bess – be not too proud.' Was his sin pride? Or was it malice? She remembered Martin's frown when she mocked her poor would-be suitors at table.

She heard shouting and laughter from the street and looked down. Near the corner where Stillman Street joined Vauxhall Street stood two men and women. Stood, or rather staggered, for all were drunk.

It was a common sight, drabs from the port waylaying sailors or soldiers. Was lust this Matthew's sin? The sun's slanting rays lit up the jostling group. These were no sailors, but a young blade in green and yellow doublet and hose and his servant in grey. The servant's face turned for a moment towards her window. Though young, he was bald, and curving eyebrows gave his face a cunning look. Then, as though he sensed they were watched, he began to shepherd his master out of sight down Vauxhall Street with the women cursing and cackling after. The young gentleman held back a moment, and his face was lit by the sun, so that Bess recognized him. It was Ferrers.

She turned quickly from the window. The noise woke her father who gasped and groped for his handkerchief. Bess took it and wiped his wet chin. His eyes smiled a fleeting second and it came into her mind to ask him about Matthew. But something warned her not to.

'Bess, pray call Sam Fletcher and his son, and bid them bring ale.'

She found the Fletchers quietly at work in the counting house. An atmosphere of peace and calm seemed to flow around them. They rose and stood by their stools.

'My father bids you wait on him in the Broad Chamber and take a cup of ale.' They went silently while Bess went herself to draw ale from the brewhouse.

As she climbed back to the Broad Chamber she heard voices raised. She knew as she reached the door that Martin was debating with his father the sermon of the wheat and tares. This was her father's sport now, to hear the Fletchers argue.

'If some be wheat and some be weeds, then that will say the Lord did plant them only to destroy,' said Martin.

'Nay, the Lord made good and bad that the good might be made strong in striving with the bad.'

'But how may a man know his place? How may he be sure of salvation? If the Lord has made him evil to strengthen the good man, he does the Lord's work.'

'Nay,' said Samuel, ' 'tis a Jesuit's argument.'

The boy answered white-faced and passionate. 'When I see the land full of poor creatures who strive and toil, I cannot believe that there is no room for them. Why should He choose one and not the other? See, shall a rich man pass safely over when his life is a vanity, when a poor man who steals a coney may be hanged without redemption?'

Jacob broke in, 'The Lord knoweth his own. Doth not the psalm say: "Men of low degree are vanity and men of high degree are a lie"? From the middle sort shall he find his saints, for they neither rest idly in their own wealth, nor grub for the charity of others.'

Martin turned sharply.

'And doth not that same psalm say "If riches increase, set not your heart upon them"? When doth the middle sort become too great?'

He stopped in embarrassment as he saw Bess in the doorway and came forward to take jug and cup from her. Then he set them down on the table and excused himself. Jacob waved a hand to let Martin go and bade Sam Fletcher drink. Then he said:

'Thy son has good in him. Yet he's too bold in disputing with thee. How can thou allow it?'

Samuel smiled: 'How can I not? How will he learn if he but ape what I have learned, little as it is? The Lord did not make the son to be like the father, save in the will to grace.'

Jacob was sullen.

'Yet the son shall not defy the father,' he said.

Bess left them talking and went into the parlour. That much she knew then. This Matthew had defied their father. Pride and stubbornness were his sins. 'Bess, be not proud.'

But how did he defy his father? What did he do that his name might not be spoken? And, if he still lived, where was he now? She rose restlessly and went into the gallery. Down in the courtyard sat Martin, a book on his knees.

She called his name and he rose, dropping the book.

'I would ask thee a favour, Martin. Nay, do but wait and I'll come down.'

She went to her room, took out a hooded cloak, threw it on her shoulders and hurried down the stairs.

'What service may I do,' asked Martin.

'The evening's still light and the walls are yet open. Walk with me to the Hoe.'

He hesitated. 'It's not seemly for me to walk with my master's daughter.'

'Then, Master Fletcher, I'll have thee walk behind me half a pace and seem to be less than me, which you are not.'

'You mock me!'

'I' faith no,' said Bess eagerly. 'Do not think so. You are more wise than I, your family as good as mine. If custom sets you one degree below, so much the worse for custom.'

Martin took his hat from his belt and set it on his head, and followed her through the door by the warehouse. A few minutes' rapid walk took them through the Hoe Gate.

They began to mount the grassy slopes of the Hoe. At the crown of the hill a few boys wrestled and played leap-frog. No one else was in sight.

'Now that we are distant from prying ears, I'll have thee call me Bess. What I have to ask is a friend's service.'

He smiled, a red spot in his pale cheek.

'Martin. You must know that my mother is long since dead, my brother Reuben also.'

'Rest their souls.'

'So. But I have learnt that before my mother, my father had another wife and another son, Matthew. I know nothing of them and my father will say nought. He denies the name Matthew. Yet I would know more of them, not least of Matthew, who is half of my flesh.'

'It may be that thy father's silence shields thee.'

'It may be. But I am of an age to choose if I be hurt or not, no more a child to be kept from the truth.'

'And what shall I do?'

Bess stopped and faced Martin.

'Canst thou inquire about the port and of older people, prudently, of these things and bring me word?'

He hesitated.

'What is it, Martin?'

'I am divided in myself. One half of me says, meddle not in others' affairs. The other says – thou hast a right to know.'

'Then do it with but half a heart and I'll be beholden to thee.'

'Not so. Thy kindness to me cancels the debt.'

They walked back to Stillman Street, the air growing dark in the east before them.

That night Jacob Morten took ill. The doctor came and shook his head over the old man who lay, scarcely breathing, his face wax-white.

'The marvel is not that he is ill, but that he still lives. But, Mistress Morten, the end will come and 'ere too long. Expect it by the day.'

As if the old man had heard these words, next day he rose from his bed and called for his clothes. With the help of Anna and Sam Fletcher, Bess forced him back to bed and quelled his feeble protests. Next day he tried to struggle up again. Bess called Anna and had her make up a bed on a couch next to the Broad Chamber window. Then sitting near him in the window seat she read for him by the hour, pausing only to eat at mid-day.

'Where's young Martin,' demanded the old man.

'He's about the port,' said Bess evasively and went on reading till she saw her father's eyelids fall. She set the book aside and dozed lightly herself. A knock at the door woke her. She went swiftly to open and found Martin there. Fingers to lips she beckoned him in. The old man's breathing rasped on the air, then died to a murmur.

'Hast news for me, Martin?'

'After a fashion. I've been about. I've talked with old wives and seamen, and a landlord or two.'

'And . . .'

'Of Mistress Morten, thy father's first wife, have I learnt this. She was of Exeter. While thy father lay five years in prison for the faith, she and Matthew lived in a cottage behind the church. She baked pies and sold them for a living. And all do say that she was kind and good. She sang sweetly in church. Of her that is all – nay that she died of the plague these thirty years back.'

'And Matthew – what of Matthew?'

In her excitement Bess's voice rose. Her father stirred. Then he slept again.

'Of Matthew, have I good report...'

'Ah.'

'... and bad.'

'How so?'

'He was apprenticed to a merchant, Abraham Combe, who once lived in this house.'

'This house?'

'Pray lower thy voice. He, like his mother, was a sweet singer. They say that folk came to Church of a purpose to hear him sing or read the Scripture.'

Bess nodded. 'But then...'

'He quarrelled with his father and took service in a ship owned by Combe that sailed to New Spain with slaves from Africa. That much is sure. Beyond that all's in darkness, or half-light. There's talk of injury done by him to others, that he cheated and robbed others of their shares. That he came back after many years laden with gold, that he fought with a gentleman in an inn on the quay. And would have killed him too...'

'What was their quarrel?'

'It was to do with the voyage.'

'And, is there more?'

' 'Tis said he took ship again to the Darien shore and there, some say he fell overboard, some that he ran away. None knows for sure.'

'I'm in thy debt for all this, Martin.'

' 'Tis little enough.'

'Hast thou paid any man for his story? I'll repay.'

'One man did demand payment. But I told him "nay".'

'What man?'

'An old sot, one time a sailor, who did ship with Matthew Morten, so he says. But he was so in his cups who'd know if he spoke truth.'

'Bess, who's there?' called her father.

' 'Tis Martin, back from harbour.'

'Bid him come near and read for me.'

Bess closed the door behind Martin, went into the parlour and sank down into her chair. Now she knew more, but did not know whether she was glad or sorry for it. She had a hazy picture of her brother – one part angel, one part devil – a little of Martin, a little of Ferrers. One thing was sure, though. Knowing a little, she longed to know more.

From the courtyard came a loud and confused noise of crashing and shouting. She ran out on to the gallery. The door to the lane behind the house was wide open and in the courtyard Sam Fletcher and a servant struggled to hold back a third man. The man was grey-haired and dirty, his clothes in foul tatters. And he was drunk. With crazy strength he flung aside Fletcher and the servant and staggered to the gallery stairs. As he clung to the banister, his eyes fixed on Bess.

'Aye lady . . . I'll tell thee of Matthew Morten, traitor and pirate dog. He robbed his own kind, he had his own shipmates murdered.'

The servant came behind him. 'Nay, Dickon, old fellow. Be good and come with me. We'll give thee ale.'

A howl of rage burst from the dirt-streaked face. The servant was thrown off and Dickon began to struggle up the stairs, cursing and railing as he came.

The door to the Broad Chamber was flung open. In the doorway stood Jacob Morten, his white shirt clinging to his bent figure, hair wild. Behind him Martin tried to hold him back. Dickon saw him and stumbled up the last few steps to crouch like a dog a yard from Jacob.

'Drunken hound,' gasped Jacob, 'get from my house or I'll have thee beaten home.'

'I'll have justice. Thy son Matthew robbed me. Curse you, Morten.'

Jacob's mouth twisted in a spasm. His chest swelled and sank in great heaves.

'I've given thee charity, beyond thy deserts. Thou didst promise me not to name that name in this town again.'

'Then who sent that boy behind thee to poke and pry and ask of Matthew Morten?'

To Bess's horror Jacob looked round wildly, first at Martin, then at her. Then he sank to the floor.

'Man of God. Hypocrite,' snarled Dickon, and, rearing up, tried to spit at the unconscious Jacob. He lost his balance, and crashed down. Both old men lay still, one at the head, one at the foot of the stairs.

Chapter six

Bess fell on her knees at her father's side as he lay across the doorway of the Broad Chamber. Martin Fletcher knelt too and bent his head to the old man's chest. His eyes grew wide in wonder.

'He lives. His heart still beats.'

Martin and a servant carried Jacob to the couch and laid him down. The old man stirred, his breath snorted. A tiny pulse beat wildly in his temple.

'Go fetch the physician,' Bess commanded.

Voices sounded from below. Martin ran to the door and came back with a rueful smile.

'The drunk man falls like a babe. What you hear is Dickon cursing all around him. He's on his way, wondering how he came hither.' He paused. 'Thy father paid a heavy price for that man's silence.'

'I cast it away.'

He shook his head. ' 'Tis folly to buy silence. What Dickon blurts out, others hold in their hearts. Which is the worse?'

The doctor came, and went. The night passed and Jacob slept on, snoring and moaning faintly. Bess stayed at his side. Only when dawn came, did she allow Dame Anna to take her place, and slept a little.

She woke with the sun in the little window of her room and a blackbird singing nearby. Judith came in with milk in a pitcher.

'Drink this, 'tis fresh from Coppins'. Thy father sleeps easy. Death's cheated again, praise God.'

Bess stood up. She had slept in her clothes and Judith fetched her fresh ones.

'Mr Trant and that old pudding Rishworth are below in the counting house, ordering matters. Sam Fletcher and Martin are ill pleased.'

Bess struggled on with her clothes.

'Quick, lace me up. I'll go down.'

Catching up her skirts with both hands, she ran along the gallery and downstairs to the counting house. Trant and Rishworth were there indeed, Rishworth anxiously rubbing his hands. Trant, his finger raised, addressed Sam Fletcher, whose good-humoured face was strained and tense. Martin stood behind his father, his dark eyes alive with fury.

'Ye must know that now you cannot stay here. Neither you nor your son. 'Tis not your fault, Fletcher, but you must take blame for your son's deeds. His prying has brought ill on this house, struck Jacob Morten down.'

'Pray be not so quick to have my father in his grave, sir,' Bess spoke from the doorway.

Trant turned, his jaw slack.

'I was but ordering the matter as thy father might, Mistress Morten.'

Bess's voice rose. 'My father sleeps above. When he wakes I shall make all clear to him. It was I who bid Martin Fletcher seek out the truth about my brother Matthew. He was unwilling but I persuaded him. The blame is mine.'

'So . . .' began Trant.

'Further, Mr Trant, I find it ill that you act for my father in this way, when he has not made his mind known in the matter.' She softened her voice. 'See, I'll order matters with my father. Pray step upstairs and see how he does. We'll not hinder Master Fletcher and Martin in his business.'

Trant walked from the room, Rishworth ducking behind Fletcher's face showed his relief.

'Our thanks, Mistress Morten. We are well pleased with our place and would not go wandering again.'

'That you shall not,' said Bess. 'May the day never come that we should bid ye depart.'

'Amen to that,' said father and son.

Days passed and Jacob Morten slept on. After a week, his eyes opened. Bess leant over him, his lips moved but no sound came. She took a cloth and wiped sweat from his face and the eyes closed again.

As summer wore on Bess found herself grow faint from lack of sleep, uncertain meals and the heat. The smell of sickness clung in her clothes and filled her head. She longed to leave the house and ride on the slopes above Coppins' with the breeze in her hair.

Margaret Bray read her thoughts.

'Bess, take rest. Go to the farm this week. Dame Anna and I will watch over thy father.'

'I cannot. What if he should weaken?'

' 'Tis simple. I've spoken with Dame Anna. There'll be a horse ready saddled and a boy to bring thee home.'

So next morning Bess woke in her narrow bed beneath the Coppins' slated roof. The sky showed blue through the slit window and from far away came the bleating of sheep. In the yard, Crispin stood ready at the head of the chestnut, stroking his head.

She went down and called 'Ho Crispin,' then lowering her voice, 'hast thou kept shirt and breeks for me?'

'Behind the barn.'

'The fit will not be so well these days. Thou art grown tall and broad.'

'And thou more fair,' he said impulsively.

Her cheeks reddened.

'Be so kind, Sir Crispin, and lead my horse behind the wall.' She turned and ran to the barn.

When she set out the sun was already high and hot. Weeks of drought had dried out the ways, and dust rose beneath the chestnut's hooves. She halted him, and taking out a handkerchief, bound it round the lower half of her face. Then she urged the horse forward.

But there was no pleasure in the riding. The dust and haze obscured her view. She rode as in a cloud. Rounding a bend in the track she suddenly came upon two riders. Their figures wavered in the haze as they came near but she knew them – Ferrers and Dauncey. They came on swiftly, riding abreast. Bess saw there was no room to pass. She slowed her horse. Would one give way, or would they force her from the path?

Thirty yards away, Ferrers rose in the stirrups, shouted and waved her aside. A wave of heat rushed into her head. She pressed her horse forward, bending low over his neck, and he three rushed at each other like knights in some court joust. Twenty, ten yards, the hooves pounded and the dust rose till all view was lost. Then Bess found herself riding alone. She reined in her horse and looked back as the dust cleared. Ferrers was still on the track, and Dauncey dismounted. He must have given way at the last moment.

She saw Ferrers wheel his horse. She heard Dauncey shout: 'Nay Ralph, do not.'

Ferrers rode after her. Bess laughed to herself.

'We'll see who's better mounted,' and set her horse going with a cry.

But she had misjudged the distance. She had barely ridden fifty yards when Ferrers at full gallop was a length behind her.

'Stop, boy, or I'll whip thee,' he yelled.

At that moment she felt a stinging pain across her back, then her shoulders, then her face. With an effort she held her seat and brought the horse to a trot. She turned, her rage burning more than the blows. But she was alone. Ferrers had swung his horse and the two were disappearing round the bend in the track.

She rode back slowly to the farmhouse and handed back the dust and sweat covered horse to Crispin. Once in her bedroom she inspected her hurts with the aid of her glass. Two angry red stripes marked her shoulders and neck. The kerchief and her bent head had saved her face but the inward hurts were more painful.

She went down into the dairy and asked Goodie Coppin for herb ointment. 'I'd a blow from a low branch.'

The old woman shook her head. 'A young lady should not ride so,' she said meaningfully.

Later that afternoon one of Judith's younger sisters found Bess as she worked with Crispin on the chestnut.

'Oh, Miss Bess, do come. A gentleman and a lady are at the gate and ask for thee.'

'What manner of folk are they?'

'Oh, 'tis them from Dauncey Hall.'

Dauncey? Bess clawed at her hair and brushed at her wrinkled skirt as she left the stable. Just beyond the farm gate, on horseback were Dauncey, small and fair, and a girl dressed in blue, as neat and fair as he. They must be twins.

Dauncey sprang from his horse as Bess approached, and drew off his feathered hat.

'Mistress Morten, I am Hugh Dauncey, this is my sister Mary. We are neighbours after a fashion. I have seen you riding near the church.' The girl smiled, looking over Bess's hair and clothing.

'You catch me ill prepared to receive you. I was tending my horse.'

Mary's eyebrows rose.

'Why, have you no groom?' Dauncey frowned at the question. Bess chuckled and looked him in the eye.

'My groom is not well. He is hurt in my service. I must shift for myself.'

Dauncey flushed. 'It is of that that we would talk.'

'Indeed?'

'Yes. Will you ride up the hill with us?'

'My horse is not fit to ride just now.'

'Then may we walk?' Dauncey gave his hand to his sister.

45

They tied their horses to the yard gate and the three set off slowly up the hill.

'Our errand, Hugh,' reminded Mary Dauncey.

Dauncey blushed and stammered.

'Our cousin . . . Ralph Ferrers, son of Sir Charles and Lady Ferrers of Ancombe . . . he often stays at our house in summer. You may have seen him ride with me. Today we met your lad riding the chestnut on the lower path. Ralph shouted for him to stand aside but he rode through us. Ralph took offence, chased him and whipped him, though I told him nay.'

'Indeed,' put in Mary. ' 'Tis not meet to beat another's man, whatever the offence.'

Hugh went on seriously: 'Ralph is a proud man. He thought he did right. I said he did wrong.'

'What should he have done?'

'Why, come to the boy's mistress that she might punish him.'

'And is that why you are come?'

Dauncey shook his head. 'I think the groom chastised enough. We came to excuse Ralph's offence to you.'

'And could he not do that himself?'

Hugh looked embarrassed. Mary answered for him. 'Our Ralph admires you, Mistress Morten, and he fears to beg your pardon.'

Bess threw back her head and laughed. Mary's eyes grew large.

'I spoke not in jest.'

'I do believe. 'Twas unmannerly of me to laugh,' said Bess. 'I did but think how strange a way to show his admiration – to beat my groom.'

Mary and Hugh joined her laughter.

'You've a ready wit, Mistress Morten. 'Tis a pity we've not met before. Life here at Dauncey can be dull,' said Mary.

'Well, we must meet again,' said Bess. 'If you should come to Plymouth, call on us in Stillman Street.'

They had reached the top of the hill, the pasture land

lay below them, hazy in the sunshine. All was still and the air heavy.

Hugh said: 'We must be frank, Miss Morten. Our family is of the old – the Catholic faith. My father sheltered a Jesuit priest and was banished from the realm for five years. A friendship between our families would not be welcomed by your kin.'

'My father,' said Bess, 'is of the new faith.'

'A Puritan,' broke in Mary.

'Those that would give offence would call him Puritan, as some call others papists,' said Bess.

Mary reddened.

'My father,' Bess went on, 'was in prison for five years. So we are quits on that score.'

Hugh nodded. 'These things are much misunderstood. Many hate us for they fear Spain. They think we'd betray the realm.'

'And Catholics would not?' queried Bess, half ironically.

Hugh clenched his teeth. 'My father stood to arms thrice when invasion threatened.' He calmed a little. 'Mistress Morten. I speak but for us. We are for the old way – to each his own, duty and reward. The man to serve – the master to rule justly, the priest to care for our souls and God to watch over all.'

'And let not ranting weavers and prating merchants come between,' added Mary.

'My father's a merchant and the kindest man I know a weaver,' said Bess mildly.

A silence hemmed them in as they walked down the slope. They halted where the Daunceys' horses were tied up and looked awkwardly at one another. Slowly all three began to smile. Bess held out her right hand. Hugh bowed over it.

'We shall be friends, despite all?'

'Why not?'

As they rode away Mary turned and called, 'God bless thee, Bess Morten.'

Bess watched them out of sight and then turned into the yard. As she did so she saw a black horse standing saddled by the farmhouse door. A boy stood by the horse – the boy from Stillman Street.

Goodie Coppin appeared in the doorway.

'Oh, Bess, poor child. Thy father – he's dying.'

Chapter seven

Bess turned to the lad from Stillman Street.

'Is thy horse fresh?'

'He's rested half an hour.'

'I'll ride him back then.'

'I'll change the saddle, Mistress.'

'Not so.'

Bess ran for the barn where Crispin's clothes were hidden. She tore off her skirt and bodice so savagely they ripped. But she cast them aside on the hay and slipped on shirt, breeches and woollen hose.

As the others stared, she climbed swiftly on to the horse's back and rode full tilt from the yard.

Half an hour's hard riding brought her to the town walls, flushed and sweat-drenched, her face streaked with dust. Her cap had fallen off and her hair hung over her eyes. She wasted no more time, but clattered through the Old Town Gate, and in a few moments had reached Stillman Street. Breathlessly she flung off the horse, ran in through the yard and rushed upstairs to the Broad Chamber. The room was full. Trant and Rishworth and their wives, the doctor, the minister from St Andrews, Anna, Margaret, Judith, Tom and Will Curnock, who must have come straight from the harbour. Near the window, apart from the others, stood the Fletchers. Trant stepped forward.

'What is it, lad?'

But Bess ignored him, pushed to the bedside and knelt

near her father, who now lay quite still, head held up by the pillows. She leaned close to his face and whispered,

'Father.'

The eyes fluttered open. The pupils swelled like water rings when a stone is thrown. A strange sound rose from his throat and his hands stretched out to grasp her shoulders.

Jacob's eyes, now fully open, searched the face before him, sweat-grimed and hot, the tumbled hair. Then slowly a smile crept round his mouth. The lips began to form a name. He gasped but no sound came out.

'Father,' Bess whispered.

Jacob's hands ran feebly down the grey shirt sleeve, fingering the coarse cloth.

Then he said, so clearly that all the room heard.

'Thou shalt read for me, lad. I've slept well. Get the Book, lad. What, lad? Why starest thou so?'

There was a movement near the window. Martin stood near her, holding out the Bible.

'What shall I read, Father?' Bess's voice trembled.

'Why, the 112th. Read that.' His voice rose, 'Thou shalt know my meaning. Read.'

Bess took the Bible. Tears blinded her, she could not find the place.

'Come lad, why wilt thou not read?'

'Praise ye the Lord. Blessed is the man that feareth the Lord.'

Quietly Martin began to speak the verses behind her. His voice slowly filled the quiet room. But Jacob's eyes were on Bess. The grip on her shoulders was painful.

'Wealth and riches shall be in his house and his righteousness endureth for ever . . .'

'Aye, lad, mark that,' gasped Jacob.

'A good man showeth favour and lendeth. He will guide his affairs with discretion . . .'

'Mark that, lad.'

'He hath dispersed . . . he hath given to the poor . . .'

'Aye, lad.' Jacob's voice rose, drowning Martin's. 'Thou wast wrong to chide me that accepted money from other's hands in the Lord's service. Thou didst wrong to rebuke me.'

Bess heard Rishworth's awestruck voice.

'His mind wandereth. He doth believe it is Matthew he sees'.

'Is that not so, lad?' Jacob gazed blindly into Bess's face.

'Father,' the cry was wrenched from Bess as the old man's hands gripped like talons.

'Fear not, lad.' Jacob's hands loosed their hold. He drew Bess's head gently into the crook of his neck and ruffled her hair.

'Take my blessing, lad. Take my blessing. Pray for thy mother and me. Aye, and see to Reuben, and little Bess ... little Bess ...'

The body shuddered, the arms tightened then fell back. The faint pulse in his temple ceased to beat.

Anna drew Bess away as the minister came forward, and led her into her own bedroom. Vaguely Bess felt hands remove the stained clothing. She felt the touch of bedclothes on her skin. Then she slept.

She slept in a fevered haze for nearly a week. Over her sleep drifted faces – Judith, Margaret, Martin and his father, Trant. And among them all was an unknown face, dark, young, like her own, that face her father had seen when he died, that was hers yet was not – that of her lost brother Matthew.

On the fifth day, by an effort of will, she rose to follow her father's body to the church. A great crowd came there and the church rang with their singing. Those who had known her father came and pressed her hand and went away. She saw them and she did not see.

But amid the crowd one face caught her eye and held it for a second, a beautiful proud face framed in chestnut brown hair, that stared into hers then suddenly vanished into the crowd.

The period of mourning that followed was torture to Bess.

She recovered from the shock of her father's last day. She ate, slept, read, roved silently from room to room. If anyone spoke to her, she answered briefly as though she had not heard. She longed to sit astride her horse again, or to sit in the prow of a boat, sails filling with the wind as it crossed the Sound. But she could not leave the house.

If her body was kept in, her mind roved wildly, leaping from one thought to another. She tried to calm herself by thinking and planning what should become of her father's business now that he was gone. Twice she rose from her seat in the Broad Chamber to go and speak to the Fletchers in the counting house. But she knew it was too soon for this.

Once she sat down and wrote letters answering those who sent words of sympathy. Among the letters was a brief note from Mary Dauncey and her brother. She wrote back and promised that one day before long they would go riding together.

Each evening as the sun went down and she sat in the window seat, her thoughts turned to the mystery at the centre of her life, which deepened the more she penetrated it: that of Matthew. Matthew who sang and prayed so sweetly. Matthew who robbed his shipmates, Matthew who fought in taverns and nigh slew a gentleman, Matthew who rebuked his father, Matthew who had killed his own mate, Matthew who vanished to the coast of Darien Gulf.

And all this happened before she was born, even before Reuben was born. Did not someone say thirty years ago? Matthew must now be fifty or more. Could he be alive? And if alive, where was he – in pirate stronghold or Spanish prison, or among the wild men of Terra Firma? She must know more, but how?

She turned to the oak chest, opened it and picked a book at random. The Broad Chamber was in near darkness but the sun still gave light in the window. She opened the volume and found it was the poems which had alarmed Margaret Bray, that day long ago.

The door creaked faintly. Bess jumped and peered into the dusk. But she could see nothing. All was quiet again. She shrugged away her alarm and began to read aloud where the page had fallen open.

'They flee from me that sometime did me seek
With naked foot stalking in my chamber
I have seen them gentle tame and meek...'

From the darkness by the door, a woman's voice took up the line,

'That now are wild and now do not remember
That sometime they have put themselves in danger...'

Bess started up from the seat and advanced a pace. Her eyes, lifted from the faintly-lit page, strained into the gloom to see a darker shape.

'Who's there?'

'Fear not, Bess Morten. I would but speak with thee.'

Bess fumbled for the candle on the window ledge.

'No need for light. I'll sit beside thee in the window.'

Anger took the place of fear. 'Madame, whoe'er you are, you have no right to come into my house and room like this.'

'Mistress Morten,' the voice was cool. 'I did intend to beg your leave to call...'

The woman sat down a yard away from Bess. Bess knew her – the same chestnut hair, fine features, haughty look, she had seen in church – and somewhere else, though where she could not recall. The woman went on.

'On impulse I came in uninvited.'

Bess spoke coolly, yet she was curious.

'How came you past the door?'

The woman smiled faintly.

'Dame Anna let me pass.'

'She had no right.'

'Haply not. Yet, she was my servant 'ere she was yours or your father's.'

'How so?'

'This house was mine 'ere it was yours, even this chest and that old volume, Mr Tottel's book of verse, which I left here by mischance.' Her voice softened. 'I had another copy once, but now it's at the bottom of the sea.'

'Madam, who are you?'

'My name is Lady Ferrers, Susannah Ferrers.'

'Ah.' That was the face she recognized. Not hers, but Ralph's.

'Lady Ferrers. I had not thought to receive you or anyone for a little while.'

'Ah, but you will. You will be a most sought-after lady.'

'You mean my wealth will be sought after?'

'Nay, if you were poor, you'd have your suitors. There's a brilliance in you that would find its way even in a dark corner.'

'Let's agree, my lady, there will be suitors. Have you counsel for me?'

'Counsel? You have a mind of your own, I know.'

'Indeed?'

'My niece and nephew told me what you said to them.'

'Did they tell you all I said?'

'In what concerned my son Ralph, they did.'

As she spoke the name, Lady Ferrers's face softened. Her hand reached out – drew back.

'Ralph is a proud, rash lad. He acts 'ere he reflects.'

'Is that so? It seems to me he's over rash in giving offence and too reflective in asking pardon.'

Lady Ferrers breathed deeply.

'He'd come to ask your pardon, but first he'd know how he would be received. He fears a rebuff.'

'Rash, but a diplomat.'

'You mock him 'ere you've met him face to face.'

Bess's hand rose to touch her neck where the whip had fallen.

'I know more of him than you think, my lady. I saw him when he saw me not, down there with his servant making merry in Vauxhall Street.'

Lady Ferrers looked uneasy.

'He's wild now, but he would settle. Our manor at Ancombe needs a firm hand, small as it is.'

'Such as a merchant's daughter and her dowry might supply?'

The pale lips tightened.

'Lady Ferrers. We have met in a strange manner. The matter of our talk I'll hear more of, no doubt. This much I'll say, for what it's worth. I think not to marry – yet.'

'You'd reject my son's suit?'

'I would not say "yea" or "nay" to any man. I would be left alone.'

Lady Ferrers rose. Her voice had a slight tremor in it.

'I have pride too. I humbled it to beg a favour of a girl. But Ferrers pride is nought to Morten pride.'

Bess rose. 'Why are you angry? You came secretly, that we might speak truth to one another. Let our families be friends and let the future bring what it may.'

'Friends. That's too much. Kin we are – and enemies. An alliance is all there might be.'

'Kin?'

'Aye, of a sort.'

Bess sat down. 'Lady Ferrers, I beg you tell me what this means.'

Lady Ferrers remained standing at the window.

'My father Abraham Combe was one of this town's merchants. Next in wealth to men like Hawkins. He traded from this house and here we lived. Jacob Morten, pikeman turned preacher, martyr of the faith, jailed for smuggling

English Bibles in Queen Mary's time, enjoyed my father's friendship and charity. So did his son Matthew . . .'

'Ah,' breathed Bess, 'what of Matthew . . .'

Lady Ferrers stared.

'Strangely like you in looks – and pride. But you are wealthy, he was poor. He worked in the counting house below, sailed in my father's ship, selling slaves across the Atlantic . . .'

'This much I've heard.'

'He loosed the cargo, let them run away. He robbed us of the profit of the voyage. All that my father ventured was lost.'

'Why did he do it?'

'Revenge.'

'Revenge?'

Lady Ferrers laughed. 'He would have wed me, but he was a timid wooer. He had a book of poems at my hand. When he discovered I would wed Charles Ferrers, he cast the book into the sea, and freed the slaves. He ruined my father, cast away my dowry. Aye, and would have slain Charles too.'

Bess asked wonderingly 'How did this apprentice boy grow to be such a roaring blade?'

Lady Ferrers shrugged.

'He had his schooling among the pirates and savages of the Darien shore and grew to be like one of them. For all I know or care, he's with them still.'

'You care not, but your wrath's still hot.'

'Like son like father. The preacher turned merchant, he dealt in stinking fish and got spice and silk therefrom. The father . . .'

'My father . . .'

'Thy father, your father, married my cousin, without dowry.'

'Was that unfair?'

'Aye, in its place, he bought this house from me when my

father died, lock, stock and barrel, for a good price – for him and not for me.'

'Thy father drove no hard bargains?'

'He drove them not with widows and orphans. Our poverty became your father's wealth.'

'And you'd have it back. You'd have me make amends?'

Lady Ferrers gave no answer. She strode to the door. Bess heard the Broad Chamber door shut. She was alone in the darkness.

Chapter eight

That night Bess lay awake brooding on what she had heard and said. Had she been wise to answer so boldly? How easily, thought Bess, the sharp words came to her tongue when she felt challenged. Like flint when the steel strikes, sparks flew.

How fine, she thought drowsily, to be like Martin and his father. Not proud, not humble, but fearless, manly. So they were. She would be like them. Yet she would be womanly. Could one person have two natures in them? Baffled, she fell asleep.

And woke after midnight from a wild dream. Moonlight shone eerily through her tiny bedroom window. She felt her breath gasp and bubble in her throat. Her chest heaved. She heard her own voice call. 'I have a brother on the Darien shore,' then she slept and woke again in sunlight.

She rose, called Judith, bid her put her mourning clothes away and bring her a brighter dress. 'And my cloak and bonnet too,' she called. 'Let them bring the grey horse to the street door. He's gentle. And put my groom's gear in the saddle bag.'

Judith's face fell. 'Wilt thou to Coppins'?'

'And prithee why not?' Bess laughed. 'Nay, I had forgot. The fishers are in harbour. Judith, I'll go alone. I can't abide thy chatter with thy mother of pans and crocks and pewter and bed linen.'

'Thou'rt kind. But is my talk of marriage goods so displeasing to thee?'

'Not for thy sake, but for mine. Now that the mourning days are over, the wooing days begin. And I must smile, at least, on men I'd scarce give an eye to otherwise.'

'I heard there is a suitor for all that.'

'How so?' Bess was alarmed.

' 'Tis said letters have passed between the Daunceys and thee.'

' 'Tis said, eh? Eyes see too much and tongues say more. Go bid them bring my horse. I'll to the counting house.'

As she entered there, at first she saw only Samuel Fletcher by the door.

'Good morrow, Master Fletcher. I'll to the Coppins' for a while, but after that we'll talk in earnest of my father's business.'

Fletcher looked uneasy and then Bess saw he was not alone.

'Why, Mr Trant and Mr Rishworth. What do you here? I had not expected you.'

Rishworth squirmed. Trant fixed his eye on the wall.

'Good morrow, Miss Morten. 'Tis good to see thee well. A breath of country air will do no harm. And, as for thy father's affairs, have no more care. We'll see to them.'

'How mean you, Mr Trant? My father's affairs are mine, are they not?'

'True,' Trant's face was rigid, 'but from this time on, thy father's, that is thine affairs, are our concern, and we shall order them.'

'What does this mean?'

' 'Tis simple. We are thy guardians till thou art five and twenty...'

'Or until thou shalt wed,' said Rishworth coaxingly. 'We'll make a brave choice for thee. I'll wager my fortune 'twill take no more than twelve months.'

'Make not so light with thy goods, Mr Rishworth. I'll choose the man and name the day.'

'Thy father's will doth give us charge,' said Trant.

'My father's will! What of mine?'

'Thy will is strong,' said Trant, a sudden edge to his voice. 'Perhaps our judgement is more sure.'

'In what is my judgement lacking?'

'Mistress Morten, I'll be frank.' He turned to the Fletchers. 'Be pleased to leave us.'

The Fletchers, embarrassment on their faces, slowly walked into the courtyard, where a servant was leading through the horse for Bess. She looked at Trant.

'This concerns thy reputation, Mistress Morten.'

'Say on,' she urged him coldly.

'Two things. One thy friendship with the Daunceys – whose father, a known papist, was banished the realm.'

'And the other?'

'Thy manner of dress.'

'Dress?' Bess's voice rose.

'Just so. To ride a horse in man's attire is unfit. Already it is noised abroad . . .'

'By those same persons who made known my private letters.'

'This thing is common fame,' said Rishworth.

'Common fame,' Bess shouted. I'll give you common fame, Mr Trant, Mr Rishworth. Hark to me. Of my father's business more on my return. Of suitors, more when it suits me. Of my friends, no more. And of my manner of dress, you shall see.'

She stormed from the counting house, ran to the horse and snatched clothes from the saddle bag. She sprang up the stairs to her bedroom.

A moment later, in her borrowed boy's clothes she ran down the stairs. Before her, Trant, Rishworth, the Fletchers, the servants, stood amazed.

'I'll speak with you again, when I am ready,' she called putting her foot in the stirrup. With a heave she was mounted. A jerk of the reins and while they stared she rode out through the street door. She swung the horse at a trot through the streets to the Old Town Gate and out on to the open road. As she rode, she muttered to herself, 'I will not be gainsaid. Ferrers, Trant, they shall not thwart me.'

As though Fletcher rode beside her she turned and said, 'Martin, sweet reason suits you, it suits me not, it becomes me not, it serves me not.'

As she galloped through the Old Town Gate, the dispute in her mind burst out into open speech. 'I have a brother on the Darien shore, that doth what he chooses – on the Darien shore, mark you.'

'Where away, lad?' shouted the watch as Bess clattered past. He told his mates. 'He rides to the Darien shore.'

He yelled after her.

'Say, lad, is that by the Saltash or the Tavistock Road?'

'I'll warrant you'll need a change of horses.'

'Aye, sea horses,' laughed his mate.

She heard nothing but the voices inside her, saw nothing but her horse's ears laid flat on his head as he raced along, her heels galling his sides. At some point on that headlong, blind ride, the goaded horse turned aside, his head pulled by her nervous hands clenching and unclenching.

She had ridden half an hour and was miles beyond the town before a warning sounded in her tormented mind and she saw that she had missed her way. The track was narrowing and leading up under the edge of the moors. Below her on the right lay a village she did not know. The sun stood high above her, her galloping shadow shortened and she knew not if she rode east or west.

Alarmed she tried to slow down the beast. But the horse excited and unnerved by his treatment could not respond. His pace changed, he slipped and stumbled on the uneven track. His legs splayed in a desperate effort to hold his balance. One hoof slid in a rut, one caught in a hole in the bank. His knees bent and jarred as they hit the earth. He rolled, kicked and sprawled on the slope below the heather.

His rider, her feet kicking clear of the stirrups, flew over his head, and fell head first. One shoulder hit the ground, her head struck a rock edge. She rolled down until she was halted by a stunted bush.

The horse struggled to its feet and stood a while, shivering. He bent his head and cropped the grass around. Then he began to trot back the way he had come.

Bess lay still. In her head was a black calm and the voices were quiet.

Chapter nine

Bess opened her eyes. The earth and sky were misty grey. The sun had gone. The air was cool. She was alone. A sharp pain in her ribs told her she lay against a stone or root and she struggled to shift herself, pressing down with her hands. Her shoulders raised a few inches, then a black agony flooded her head and she sank down in darkness.

She woke again. Now there was darkness around her and within her. She did not dare to raise her head. Numbness, ache and the black pain inside her head made one. A spinning dizziness took hold of her. Then grey light came again. A breeze moved her hair and spoke to her in a faint voice: 'Get up, lad. Thou'lt perish. The dew's for maiden's beauty not for boy's.'

How strange. Now the breeze caressed her cheek. Her eyes opened, looked into two other eyes, old grey ones, veined and bleary. There was a grimed and wrinkled skin, dirty white hair. Was that the wind's face? Was it North, South, East or West? The breeze spoke again. She saw the lips move.

'Come, get up. I'll help thee.'

She struggled up, each part of her body coming into painful life as she rose – bruised ribs, numbed legs and feet. Her knees bent like cloth, she stumbled.

'Come away up the hill. I've fire and shelter.'

She felt a jacket placed around her shoulders. There was a whiff of something familiar – stables, straw and dung. An arm behind her back urged her up the slope. She climbed stiffly but with greater strength as her legs recovered their feeling.

'Come away.'

There were bushes, small trees, a shelter of branches and a fire.

'Drink this.'

A leather cup was pressed against her lips. Sour beer flowed into her mouth. She choked and coughed, but swallowed.

'Eat this.' It was an oatcake, baked or blackened in the fire, hard and tacky in parts. She ate, curled like a child near the warmth of the fire, and dozed.

Then she sat up. The sun stood high, the scent of the moors reached her on the breeze. A mile or two away were cottages and a church wavering in the heat haze.

Where was she? Who was she?

'What's thy name, lad?'

An old man sat by her, gaunt and travel stained, doublet torn, breeches tattered. The legs were bare but on the feet were ploughman's boots. About his shoulders was a cloak which had once been rich blue with a gold thread. Now it was a black-purple with wear and grime.

'What's thy name?'

'Be – ', the word would scarcely come out. Her mouth wobbled, the tongue could not hold the sound straight.

'Here, drink more. Thou'rt parched.'

Bess drank.

'Now, speak again.'

'Bess,' she whispered hoarsely.

'Aha, Ben. Good lad. Ben art thou. Well, I am Walter, Walter Carew, Knight.'

'Sir Walter?'

'H'm – a knight fallen on hard times, but not bad company, I trow. Where dost come from, Ben?'

Where? Bess looked back into her mind, but saw only blackness. She shook her head.

'From nowhere, eh? 'Twill do. But what's thy family name? Eh? No name. Well, thou'rt Ben and that will do.'

The old man stirred the fire with a stick.

'See here, Ben. In Shropshire, to the north, I have estates, fine lands, good tenants, demesne, assart and forest land. And I must hasten back to claim them.'

He shook his head.

'I've spent too long in the Queen's business in Lisbon, the Low Countries, Germany, among the Eastlanders, embassies and ambuscadoes, missions and sorties. My sword's long since broken into pieces. And if I come not soon to Shropshire, others will take my fortune clean away. Then woe to my tenants and servants. They'll be put on the road.'

Walter stopped and eyed Bess closely.

'Hast thou a case like that? Hast lost thy fortune?'

'I know not.'

'Perhaps they stole thy land and goods, and cast thee out in a stable gear?'

'Perchance.' Perchance?

'Stranger things come to pass these days. Knighthoods are sold like cabbages, cobblers buy land and gentlemen's sons are appointed to drapers. 'Tis topsy-turvy time. And they who served best, are served worst. Now, wilt come with me, Ben?'

Bess shrugged.

'We'll go to Hereford to claim my estates.'

Bess frowned.

'Thou didst say Shropshire.'

'Nay, Hereford, lad. Contradict me not. I'm older and therefore wiser. Thou'rt but a lad.'

'Nay,' said Bess firmly.

'Not a lad, eh. Thou'rt not a man, for sure, though will be some day – and a well-favoured one.'

'Nay.'

'Art a wilful boy to cross me so. Wilt anger me?'

'Nay, good Sir Walter.'

'Dost mock me now?'

'Oh nay, Sir Walter.'

'Well then. Shall we go south and seek thy fortune, or north and seek mine?'

'In Hereford, Sir Walter?'

'Nay, on my life art a wilful boy – in Shropshire.'

'I'll go with thee, Sir Walter.'

'Come then, lad. Thou shalt hold my arm till we can find thee a stout ash stave. Then haply, when I am weary, I may lean on thee a little.'

'Gladly.'

Sir Walter kicked earth over the fire, took up his staff and wrapped his cloak around him.

'Sir Walter. What of thy jacket?'

'Keep it, lad. 'Tis cold o' nights. Come on, let's away.'

That night they slept in a farmer's barn, leaving before the dogs began to bark. Next night they slept in a shepherd's hut on a windy treeless hill. And on the next day they slept under a bush. Bess lost count of days and numbered the hours only by her stomach. And her stomach learned to grumble less on days when meals were fewer and smaller.

Sometimes they caught a little rabbit, or a fish from a stream. Sir Walter was no skilful poacher, nor was Bess any better. But roots, berries, mushrooms and herbs, he did know and taught Bess – what to pick and what to leave. When they could not poach or pick their dinner, they begged it. Sir Walter would approach a farmhouse door, leaving Bess at the gate.

'Now Ben, lad. Look hungry. Let thine arms hang down and thy mouth droop open, so. 'Tis excellent.'

At the door, Sir Walter would plead, turning round to gesture at Bess's forlorn figure. Sometimes they were brought in, sat by the kitchen range and fed on porridge.

The good wife would ruffle Bess's hair and look with pity at her, while servants listened curiously to the sad tale of Sir Walter Carew's estates in Shropshire, or Sir Walter Villiers's estates in Derbyshire, or Sir Walter Fitzherbert's estate in Lincolnshire. Each time the story altered a little. Perhaps, Bess thought, this was why they tacked about the country, now east, now west. Only two things never altered He was always Sir Walter and he was always kind to her.

Sometimes they would be turned away without a groat or a bite. Sometimes they fled with the dogs after them. Then Sir Walter would shake his fist at a safe distance and shout 'Puritan rogues.'

Indeed they might have starved. But they could depend on rough charity from fellow wanderers on the way.

'Mark you, Ben. Have a care! There are three and twenty different sorts of wandering rogues, Abraham men who are touched in the wits, jarkmen who forge licences to beg, counterfeit cranks who can pretend illness, break their legs at will, foam at the mouth to order, bully boys thrown out of the Queen's service when war's over. There are many sorts and not all of them honest as we are.'

'Nay,' answered Bess, 'that I trow.'

Sir Walter avoided towns and villages like the plague.

'Ben, lad. Come not into the hands of authority – beadle, constable, church-warden, Sheriff – damnable Turks and Puritans every one. They have two score laws for every offence and every one is punished by a whipping or a branding.'

A light shone briefly in Bess's dark mind. 'They crop men's ears, for writing books without a licence.'

'Right and proper,' grunted Sir Walter, 'so they deserve – Puritan rogues who fox the Queen's subjects so.'

'Are all men Puritans, they who punish and they who offend?'

'So they are, Ben. All that are not true and loyal like thee and me.'

One night they lay under the stars. Sir Walter looked up and pointed.

'See what harm men do, meddling with God's laws. Once

each star sat in its place, ring upon ring outward from earth, even unto the seventh heaven where our Lord doth sit with his angels. Now comes one and says "Nay, not so. The sun is fixed and all move round it like a maypole." Canst thou feel the earth move, Ben? And yet others say "The sun is fixed, the earth is fixed, and some stars move. And some circle and some loop."

'Now how can that be? But I'll tell you this. When all's confusion in heaven, all's at odds on earth. God rest thee, Ben. Good night.'

'Good night, Sir Walter.'

Bess woke in half darkness. Her body throbbed. A dull ache spread around her spine. Her monthly change was at work in her.

'Heigh-ho,' she murmured. 'I'd almost forgotten I was a maid.' She moved away from Sir Walter's side for a while and then returned and lay looking at the stars. The old man stirred.

'Sir Walter,' she said, 'canst see the Great Bear?'

'Aye, what of it?'

'It moved. Before 'twas over there, and now 'tis lower in the heavens.'

'Nay, lad, 'tis thy wits that wander.'

They slept again and suddenly awoke. Two men in smocks, with billhooks in their hands, stood over them. One kicked Sir Walter.

'These are the rogues who stole the mistress's napkins from the line for sure.'

Sir Walter scrambled up. 'Dog, if I had my sword in my hand, you'd pray for mercy.'

The man jabbed Sir Walter in the belly with the handle of his hook. The old man sat down, winded.

Bess was jerked to her feet and prodded before them. Sir Walter struggled after them, shouting.

'Hurt not the lad. 'Twas I who did it.'

They were led to a farm outhouse and thrust inside. A

farm maid slipped them a crust apiece, but otherwise they fasted. In the afternoon they were marched half a mile to the village and pushed into the church vestry. Around a table sat four men, soberly dressed. One spoke.

'These are the rogues, Master Beadle?'

'Aye, sir,' said a stout red-faced man, who stood by the door.

'Thou, greybeard. What's thy name?'

'Sir Walter Baskerville, of Baskerville Hall in Norfolk.'

'Art a long way from thy lands. Take him, thrash him and set him on the road east. See he gets to the next parish and comes not back to us.'

Sir Walter was marched out. Bess tried to follow, but one of the labourers held her back. She bit his hand and he cuffed her head till it rang.

'Now lad, what's thy name?'

'Ben.'

'Ben what?'

Bess shook her head.

A word formed in her mind's darkness.

'Ben Mor . . .'

'Ben Moore, eh. Of what parish?'

Bess shook her head. A man at the table called and the beadle came back into the vestry.

'Is the old rogue on his way?'

'Aye and warmly, Master.'

'See Master Beadle. Can you board this boy till hiring day, then take him to Wimberley Market? Someone will take him for the year.'

The beadle beckoned to Bess. As they went out the churchwardens were busy with other matters and did not look at her.

On hiring day, the beadle roused Bess at six.

'Come lad, look sharp. We'll to Wimberley Market.'

'Sir, where's Wimberley?'

'Why, in Wiltshire county. Thou must surely have come from far off. Canst not remember thy home parish?'

Bess shook her head.

'Well, lad. Home's where the heart is. So set thy heart on Wimberley.'

A six-mile walk left Bess footsore and thirsty and the noise in the market place thronged with farmers, farm servants, and animals, bewildered her. The beadle pushed into the throng, dragging her behind him. By the market cross stood the constable at his table, badge in jacket and staff in hand. The beadle grunted 'good morrow'. Both men looked at Bess.

'Master Drayton over there wants a boy to train up. He's tired of serving maids and men who come and go.'

The constable pointed to a broad man in a green jacket, who slowly scratched his half-bald head as he looked the crowd over. The beadle approached him.

'Master Drayton?'

'Aye.'

'We've a parish lad. You may hire him for a twopenny fee.'

'Where does he come from?'

'We know not, he knows not.'

'Aye. Bring him over. What's thy name, lad?'

'Ben Moore, sir.'

'What's thy parish?'

Bess shook her head.

'See my horse, over by the inn. The roan gelding. Go stand by him, wait for me there. Give him to eat of his bag but not too much.'

Bess saw to the horse and sat and dozed in the late autumn sunshine while men came and went. One man gave her a cup of ale which went quickly to her head. She fell asleep to wake when she felt the shove of a boot against her leg. She looked up and saw a thin, bent, grey-haired man.

'Art thou Ben Moore?'

'Aye.'

'Well, I am Derrick, Master Drayton's man. He's away with his horse. We shall go after.'

Bess got up dully and followed Derrick. Her head felt light and her footsteps wavered. Derrick dug into his pocket and passed her a lump of cheese. 'Eat up, lad. 'Tis five miles to Drayton's.'

It was dark when they reached Derrick's cottage.

Bess could only stagger to the straw-filled sack that lay in one corner and fall asleep. She woke the next day to the sound of hens roosting in the rafters. A pig lay grunting at her feet. Derrick sat at the plain wooden table, loaf and cheese before him.

'Hey up, lad. Too much sleep maketh a man poor. Come, eat quickly, then we'll out.'

Outside the morning air was keen and chill. There was frost in the air. Bess thought of Sir Walter and wondered where his beaten old body had lain this past fortnight.

'Come, lad. We'll harness up. We're to plough the ten-acre.'

'Horses?'

'Aye lad, no oxen yoke for Master Drayton.'

Bess led out the horses. They were a powerful, well-fed pair. Derrick looked sharply at her.

'Art handy with horses, lad. They like thee well.'

He rattled on cheerfully as they walked the pair down the slope to a field screened by a row of elms. There the horses were put to the plough. Bess stared at it.

'Art astonished, Ben? 'Tis a two-share plough. Master did have the blacksmith make it to his own plan. It does the work of two. Now go thou to the head, and we'll begin from here.'

'Why so?'

'Why lad, sheltered behind the trees we may take our ease from time to time. Go gentle, go steady, go well, say I. If the plough doth twice as much, then we must do half, so that all's even, eh lad?'

He began to sing.

*'Oh I can plough
And I can sow
And I can reap
And I can mow
And I can doe
My master too
If he turn his back.'*

'Steady, lad, steady. This side must be well ploughed.'

'Why this side and not that?'

'If thou must know, Ben, and I see thou'rt a lad who will know, from here to that crook in the hedge did all once belong to me.'

'Nay, how was that?'

'My old dad, Master Drayton's father and six others did have the manor land hereabout. The lord would brave it at court and got himself in debt. So when the leases fell due, he sold them. Up went the rents and I for one could not pay the rent. But Master Drayton could. So had he my land as well.

'Next he swapped some land on the farther side, for that strip that lay between his and mine, and joined the two together. Next he did cozen his neighbour to the north over their boundary marks, and the fool did go to court. And when the poor soul had beggared himself to the lawyers, why Master Drayton bought the lot.

'So he hedged the land about to mark what he owned and shelter his beasts from the wind. Then did he say, right cheerily, "Come be my man, Derrick".'

'Why,' burst out Bess, 'he's a rogue.'

'So he be – but a good yeoman. He scatters not his seed like others do, but dibs it four seeds in a hole. Twelve bushels to the acre he has when others get eight. When they go down, he goes up. But I care not.'

'Why not?'

' 'Tis plain. He'll grow rich. His children will fly high. His wealth will go to marry his daughters to gentlemen, to send his son to school and make him an esquire. His son will go up to London and brave it round the town and Drayton's grandson will be as poor as Derrick. 'Tis the way of the world.'

Bess grew warm with the trudging up and down and without thought began to throw off her coat.

'Nay, lad,' called Derrick. 'Keep thy sweat in thy jacket. Take it steady. 'Tis a long way to sundown.'

At sunset, Bess dragged herself on to her straw sack and slept till Derrick dragged her up at sunrise. And so it went on, an endless wheel of dawn and sunset, rising up and going to bed, in mist, frost, hail and bright days. Some nights she dropped into sleep like a stone into a well. Some nights she twisted and babbled in dark dreams.

One morning as the first snows fell, Derrick woke her and said:

'What ailed thee in the night, Ben? Thou didst cry aloud.'

'What did I say?'

'I have a brother on the Darien shore.'

A single ray of light pierced the darkness in her mind.

'My name's not Moore,' she said.

'What is it then?'

'I know not.'

'Well, Master No-Moore. Let's out to the barn and do some-more,' chuckled Derrick.

'Say, if thou likest not Master Drayton and would go elsewhere, how then?'

'Why on hiring day I go and see what other master will have me.'

'What, wait twelve months?'

'Aye, lad, twelve months we serve.'

'How if you'd go away?'

'Away? I understand thee not.'

'To another place.'

'Nay, we bide, each man where he was born. Unless he get a paper from the justice.'

'Why, 'tis servitude.'

Derrick stared. 'Thy dream's upset thy wits, Ben. That was a wilful speech.'

Bess muttered to herself. 'Twelve months and then a change of master.'

Derrick shook his head. 'Hey lad, let's be off. Go thou and fetch hay from the barn for the horses.'

Bess pushed back the barn door. There was a sudden rustling. She plucked up a fork and stirred the straw vigorously.

Startled, Bess gasped : 'Who's there?'

From amid the straw rose a rake-like figure, tattered but unmistakable.

'Sir Walter!'

Chapter ten

Sir Walter laid a finger on his lips.
'Hush. Didst think I'd forsake thee, Ben?'
Bess looked at him in wonder.
'I've come to take thee with me, lad. I know of a place where we may lie warm and snug, much used by wandering folk – all honest rogues.'
'Where does it lie?'
'Eastward lad, where else?'
'Shropshire lies to the north.'
'Shropshire – fiddle faddle, lad. 'Tis Gloucestershire we seek. Our haven lies within a sniff of the port of Bristol.'
Derrick beat on the barn door.
'Quickly, Ben. Master Drayton's about.'
'I must go now,' said Bess, 'Canst lie hidden till nightfall?'
'Right snugly.'
'I'll creep out then and meet thee here.'
'Good lad. Then we'll away.'
The day passed slowly. Derrick and Bess carried fodder for the cattle. The ground was frost-bound and Drayton, prudent man, had all his beasts under cover.
Bess drew the raw air into her lungs and blew on her chapped hands. Derrick looked glum. He hated winter. Bess's heart ached a little at the thought of leaving him, for he had been kind. But she could not stay; the answer to her questions of where and who and why could not be dug out of Wiltshire soil.

Evening came and Bess slipped outside. The night was clear and the moon was rising cold and white over the trees. She went silently over the farmyard to the barn. Sir Walter, wrapped in his threadbare cloak, waited in the shadows.

'Let's away,' he muttered.

Derrick called from the cottage, 'Ben, lad, come in. Thou'lt freeze out there.'

Bess hesitated. Sir Walter clutched her arm. 'Come.'

Together they slipped away over the fields. Behind them the dogs began to bark and a light shone from the farm.

'Haste,' said Sir Walter, his long legs stalking like a heron's over the iron-hard ground. Bess broke into a run and the farm fell behind them. By daybreak they were ten miles away and sheltering in a woodman's hut. They slept until evening, ate cheese which Bess had brought with her and when the moon came up, set out on their journey again. Now the land was more open and rolling, with long stretches of pasture with copses dotted here and there.

' 'Tis sheep country,' said Sir Walter, 'all men gone but two shepherds and a dog. We may walk in daylight if we please.'

And so they did for a day and a night, snatching an hour's sleep here and there. They passed cottages with broken roofs, lonely granges where no light nor life showed.

'No one there. The land's bought up and put to pasture. The sheep's foot turns muck to gold and where it runs, men must depart.'

'But,' said Bess, 'if the sheep drive out men, where do men go?'

Sir Walter shook his head.

'Some on the roads to beg their bread, some to the woods to lie in wait and steal, some to the towns in search of work. Some to the ports to seek their fortune.'

A grotesque shape loomed up in the moonlight.

'What's that?' asked Bess.

'An oxhead on a stake. Murrain has struck the cattle in this part and here no man comes. And we, good Ben, are near our goal. Look there.'

Ahead lay a clump of trees and the black shape of a church. A light flickered.

Bess clutched Sir Walter's arm. 'Was that a spirit?'

'Nay lad, 'tis flesh and blood, no Jack-o'-Lantern.'

'They keep late hours with their worship.'

He laughed. 'Worship!'

As they came closer Bess could see the church and the cottages were half in ruins. But from the broken rafters of the church came a curling plume of smoke. From inside came light and the sound of music.

Sir Walter took his staff and beat three times on the side door.

A drunken voice cried, 'Who's without?'

'Friends.'

After a moment the door opened, a foot appeared and a woman's face with grey, tangled hair, peered out.

'Good night, Dame,' said Sir Walter.

She cackled with laughter.

'Why, 'tis that old rascal, Walter Lee.'

'Then let him sit on his bum and freeze,' came the answer. The woman shrieked again with merriment.

Sir Walter raised his foot and pushed vigorously on the door. It flew open and the old dame fell on her back cursing.

'Forward Ben. Good morrow all. 'Tis past the witching hour,' called Sir Walter.

They stepped inside and the door grated shut. The air inside the narrow vestry was stale and foul, but it was warm. A long fire blazed in the centre and round it, men and women sat or lounged or lay and snored. Sir Walter drew Bess to the fire and they warmed themselves.

'A fine blaze.'

'Aye,' said a man on the other side of the flames, 'started with ash and continued with beech.'

Dame Joan recited:

'Ash wet, ash dry,
'Fit for a queen to warm her slippers by.'

But the knight ignored her. He addressed the first speaker with dignity. 'Ash we saw by the road as we came. But where did you find seasoned beech?'

Two men, holding pipe and drum, threw themselves about with laughter.

'The good folks here have no use for their pews these days. They no longer warm their seats with their backsides, so we have leave to warm our backsides with their seats.'

Behind the fire a giant of a man with thick curled head, his half-naked body part covered with a sleeveless sheepskin jacket, stood up.

'Pay no heed to this rabble rout, Walter. Who's the lad?'

'My good friend Ben.'

'And what does thy good friend Ben, save help thee play the counterfeit knight?' asked old Joan.

'My friend Ben is a traveller.'

'Ain't we all!'

'Ben is a traveller with a purpose. He has a brother on the Darien shore, he fain would meet with.'

A red-headed man thrust his head forward.

'What is thy brother then? A Don?'

Bess shook her head.

'A Moskito savage or a Carib, then?'

'Mock not the boy,' said the man in the sheepskin.

'If he's neither Don nor savage, he must be 'Maroon.'

' 'Maroon, what manner of beast is that?' asked the drummer.

'Why,' said Redbeard, ' 'Maroon doth signify Cimaroon or as the Dons say Cimarrones, they who dwell in the mountains.'

'Goats or sheep?' said the piper.

'I'll stap that reed down thy gullet, if thou holdst not thy peace,' retorted the sailor. 'Cimaroons, lad, are blackamoors who have escaped the Spaniards.

'They are passing fierce and cruel. They do make carbonado of the Dons if they can seize them. And if he's none of those, then he must be a renegado.'

'Have a care,' said Sir Walter. 'Wilt say Ben's brother is a turncoat, a traitor?'

'A truce to this quizzing,' roared the man in sheepskin.

'A friend of Walter's a friend of mine. Come sit here, boy, and taste this stew.'

'What do you cook, Ned?'

'What else doth walk hereabouts, but sheep and men. And 'tis no man.'

' 'Tis mutton stew.'

'Aye by courtesy of my Lord of Darchester, who will not miss the one, having ten thousand more.'

The piper and drummer struck up a tune as Ben and Sir Walter sat down.

> *'Dear Mr Pratt,*
> *Thy sheep are very fat*
> *And we thank thee for that,*
> *We leave you the skin*
> *To pay for thy wife's pins*
> *And you may thank us for that.'*

'Now, Ben,' roared Ned, 'meet thy new friends. I'm Ned, charcoal burner, on my way to Worcestershire with my mate Colin and our good lady Joan. We were in Forest of Dean and lay as snug as swine in muck. But it's decreed we may not burn for fifteen miles around the coast.'

'Aye,' said Sir Walter, 'they'd have the timber for ships to fight old England's battles.'

'Hm,' grunted Ned 'and they'd have our charcoal to smelt iron for cannon to fight old England's battles, too.'

A lank-haired gaudily dressed young man spoke up. 'I've heard there is a secret way to smelt iron with sea coal. Thy day is over, Ned.'

'Never,' said Ned, 'sea coal does not give the heat. Why, today with good charcoal and a water bellows, men smelt iron by the ton. That well-versed fool there, Ben, who knows everyone's trade better than his own, was a student. But he lived so well his creditors knew him better than did his professors. So now he's on the drum.'

'The drum?'

'The high road.'

'Poor lad,' screeched Joan. 'He doth but suffer from want like all the rest of us.'

'Want of what?'

'Want of wit.'

'Nay, lack of gold.'

'Money, 'tis a curse,' said Sir Walter. 'They that have it not will have. They that have it will have more. In happier times, good masters dwelt upon their land, and saw their folk were fed. But now they sell their land to bakers and fly to court. For dirt is gold these days.'

'Money,' said the student, 'sets free the foot of man. Land ties him down.'

'Money,' said Sir Walter, 'turneth the land upside down, till no man knoweth good from evil. As good Sir Thomas More did say in his tale of Utopia land...'

'I know it not,' said the piper, 'does it lie next thine estates in Shropshire?'

Ned raised a huge fist and bowled the piper over. He turned to Walter. 'What said Sir Thomas More?'

'*Ubi omnes pecuniis netiuntur, ibi vix unquam posse fieri ut cum republica aute iuste agatur aut prospere.*'

'Lord save us,' cackled Joan, 'he has swallowed the book and wears the binding on his back.'

'What doth it mean?'

'Ask the student there.'

The student hiccuped and shook his head. The piper jeered. 'All he did learn is fashions out of France.'

Bess had a sudden vision of a sunlit window, an oak chest, books leather-bound. As in a trance she saw one open and she spoke out loud.

'Where money beareth all the stroke it is hard and almost impossible that there the weale publique may justly be governed and prosperously flourish.'

'Why, Ben, thou art a scholar,' cried Ned. 'Have drink from my cup.' He gripped Bess's shoulder in a bear hug.

'Ned,' said Sir Walter. 'Ben and I will lay us down. We've journeyed far.'

'Well enough. But take your places near the door. All others are claimed.'

The last Bess saw, as she fell asleep, was the student capering round the fire with old Joan while the piper and drummer played.

She woke to cold daylight streaming through the broken roof. From the door above her came thunderous knocking.

'Open up, open up.'

She woke Sir Walter. He clambered to his feet, pulling his cloak around him.

'Ben, we must fly. 'Tis the Sheriff's men.'

Chapter eleven

As Bess started up and the sleepers slowly came to life, the vestry door was smashed in and men with drawn swords rushed through. Sir Walter threw himself in front of Bess and went over like a skittle. A sword point scored Bess's ribs and flung her bleeding to the floor. The others, half dazed, put up no fight. The soldiers ranged them against the wall and searched them to the screams and curses of old Joan. A man in black cloak and plumed hat strode in.

'Let that old beldame cease her yowling and see to the old man and the youth.'

Bess looked up to see Joan bending over her, grey locks hanging down. The old woman plucked open Bess's shirt to get at the cut, pulled away the kerchief inside. Her eyes widened.

'Why, 'tis no cove, 'tis a mort, as I live – a maid.' She looked behind her, then whispered.

'Take my counsel then, say nought. Where you are bound, you'll fare better as man than maid.'

She inspected Bess, then fastened up the shirt.

' 'Tis a scratch. The blood's stopped flowing already. Now I'll go and see how fares Walter, poor old devil.'

Bess got to her feet. The bailiff pointed to the captives in turn.

'The charcoal burners and the old hag there have licence to travel through the land, the sailor too has licence to beg; aye, and the student too, though I doubt it's forged; drummer and piper are kicked out from Bristol. If we send them back, they'll kick them out again.'

'Let them go forward then. Send a man to ride with them to the next hundred, and see they do not double back. What of the boy?'

'I know not, sir. The old villain plays the counterfeit gentleman. The lad must be his partner. What's thy name, boy?'

'Ben Moore, sir.'

'What parish?'

Bess shook her head.

'No matter, sir. Where he'll go, 'twill make no odds.'

' 'Tis well, then,' said the Sheriff. His eye took in the vestry and he wrinkled his nose.

'Wait, though. There's mutton in that pot; go get them back. I'll have a life for that. Someone shall dance the hemp jig for that sheep.'

Old Joan croaked, 'No need of that, my lord. Your life is here.'

All turned to look, where Sir Walter lay on the floor. Bess stared in horror and threw herself down beside him.

His face and lips were wax-white but the bleary eyes still knew his friend.

'Aye, sir,' said the bailiff. 'He'll counterfeit no more.'

As though he heard the words, Sir Walter smiled faintly at Bess as she bent over him.

'Well, Ben lad,' he whispered, 'I'll find my estate at last and if they move me not, I'll lie in consecrated ground.'

'Say not so,' whispered Bess.

'Aye, lad, thy counterfeit Sir Walter has done with it all . . .'

'Nay, not counterfeit. My very true Sir Walter.'

Bess kissed the dirt-streaked forehead. He smiled again and died.

'There's sentiment among rogues, sir,' grinned the bailiff; the Sheriff shrugged.

'I'll home to breakfast. Let the beldame go find her charcoal burners.'

'She's gone, sir.'

'Then take the lad to Captain Yarwood. And cheat me not on the fee. Aye and send a man to bury the old rogue.'

'Your servant, sir,' the bailiff said. The Sheriff, followed by men-at-arms, marched out leaving the two of them.

The bailiff looked at Bess.

'Art a well-spoken young knave, and a pretty lad under that dirt. Whence did thou come, what parish?' he asked suddenly.

Bess looked blank. A name hovered like a moth in the back of her mind, then vanished into dark.

'Thou truly dost not know thy birthplace. Strange.'

'Where am I bound, sir?'

'Why, the Americas, lad. Captain Yarwood waits at the Unicorn in Darchester. He lacks stout young men for his venture to Virginia land.'

'Say, sir, does that lie near the Darien shore?' asked Bess eagerly.

'Ask the skipper, I know nought of distant waters. I've sailed to the Low Countries. Sick as a dog I was.'

'Is it far to Darchester?'

'Four miles to the Unicorn. Then ten miles down to Bristol. After that God knows.'

Bess trudged behind the bailiff's horse across the bleak countryside, white with snow under a grey sky.

It was noon when they reached the town and he lost no time in handing Bess over to the Captain in the inn parlour. Money changed hands and the bailiff nodded. A swift movement of his hands divided the coins, some in the left pocket, some in the right.

'This is Ben Moore, of any parish you like, Captain. He's had schooling, but kept bad company. He wants a father's hand.'

Yarwood, a gross double-chinned man, whose laced collar hung open, grunted.

'A father's hand he shall have, where all sons need it, at the seat of wisdom.'

The bailiff chuckled and went out. The Captain looked Bess over.

'Sir.'

'What is it?'

'The bailiff said you sailed for Virginia.'

'The bailiff saith too much. But 'tis true. When we've our full complement of bold young men, like thee, and the weather's kinder, we shall set sail. Farewell old England, hail Virginia, Sir Wat Raleigh's new paradise across the wide sea.'

'Does our way pass by the Darien shore, sir?'

'Why wilt thou know?'

'I have a brother that doth lie there.'

The Captain's stare grew sharper. Bess added hastily, '. . . and he's neither Don nor Carib, Cimaroon nor renegado.'

'Then, by the mark, what is he? What's his name?'

'Matthew . . .' the name burst out, astounding Bess.

'Matthew Moore, eh? Well, 'tis nought to me. Well Ben, I'll tell thee this. The easterlies will carry us, God willing, to the Antilles. We'll pass New Spain to larboard and God grant us a south-westerly to carry us clear of the Mexico Gulf and through the Florida passage.'

'But what of Darien, sir?'

The Captain laughed till his double chins shook.

'Why keep a weather eye open and since thy brother's such a marvel, being neither Don nor Carib, Cimaroon nor renegado, thou'lt spot him at fifty leagues, and he'll wish thee God speed.' The Captain's laugh turned to hiccups and he wiped his chin.

'Now Ben Moore, brother of Matthew, Lord of Darien, get thee out into the yard and climb aboard the wagon there. When I've dined, we shall start.'

Bess found the wagon, with two half-starved nags hitched to it, and climbed under the sailcloth that covered it. In the dark space beneath were others.

Most were asleep though one snuffled and whined. Bess settled into the small empty space left on the boards. The air was foul under the cover, but so many were crammed there it was warm enough. An hour passed.

The wagon lurched forward and began to rock and sway over the rutted yard and out on to the road. The motion awoke the sleepers, who drowsily cursed and shoved each other, then one by one snored again.

When the wagon stopped at last, Bess drew the canvas flap aside and looked out. In the winter dusk she could see rigging and masts against the sky. There was a powerful reek of tar and tallow and a background of seagull cries.

A heavy hand thumped on the sailcloth.

'Get down, lubbers, all. Let's see your fine faces.'

Bess leapt nimbly down. The wagon stood on a quayside not more than ten yards from the ship. Beyond the wagon, between the sleepy figures who now climbed from the wagon, and the road stood a line of men, sailors in stiff canvas jackets and breeches. Some held lanterns, others swung their arms and slapped their shoulders. Bess felt the cold suddenly strike her after the moist warmth of the wagon and she shivered.

Her eyes wandered to the ship. She found herself sizing it up — perhaps six score feet long, nine or ten score tons.

'Now, mark that lad,' she heard Yarwood say. 'He's a rare one. We shall need to keep an eye on him. Well, Master Moore, what do you think of our flyer?'

'She's no flyer Captain Yarwood, though I trow she's handy enough. But not for the Americas — shipping casks to Burgundy's more her mark.'

The sailors yelled and slapped their thighs. One huge man in a red woollen cap turned to the Captain.

'He's no parish sweeping, Skipper. He'll make a sailor.'

'Nay, he's for another way — Virginia's plantations await him, unless perchance he leap overboard and swim a hundred leagues to Porto Bello. Now on board with all of 'em. They've cost me dear enough.'

Chapter twelve

Captain Yarwood intended to keep his ship, the *Bonaventure*, lying at Bristol for a while. He'd no stomach for the winter gales. He had got together four score colonists for Virginia, where the tobacco planters waited. But he did not expect four score to arrive there. So he wanted to make the number to five score before sailing.

The space he'd provided on the boarded-in main deck was four score feet long and twenty wide. Take away space for the long boat stowed amidships, and it gave each traveller less room than a horse stall. Now if there were five score, there'd be less space, and fever or the flux would spread the quicker. But if you sailed with more, you might arrive with more. If you started out with fewer, more might survive and you paid less for stores.

It was a very fine point, and when Yarwood supped with the merchants who shared his venture, after church on Sundays, he was ready to debate the point with all comers. He favoured ship-more, lose-more, have-more. So he was inclined to stay. His quarters in the Turk's Head tavern near the jetty were warmer and more comfortable than his quarters on the *Bonaventure*.

The main deck was warm, with the heat of 80 young bodies. There were 60 youths and 20 girls and the crew had roughly divided the area with a sailcloth. But the bigger lads soon found fault with the way the space was divided, and later the canvas was filched to patch mattresses and clothes.

Before the voyage was over the only division made was between strong and weak, and the passengers packed together as best they could in the murk of the timber cavern. Half of them had come from the highway, like Bess. Some were cottagers' sons hoping for a better life in Virginia. And some were tradesmen's children with signed indentures, sealed with the Plantation Company's seal. In their neat clothes and kerchiefs, their bundles of clean linen and keepsakes, they formed a group apart at first.

But soon, the better dressed had shared their clothing with the others. The sharing was done by others as they slept. Some disputed the shareout and there were tussles and blows. One lad had a knife-wound dressed by the ship's barber.

Some submitted with oaths and some with tears. But in the end all were alike in rags and in dirt.

And in sickness. Soon came the first signs of the flux as mouldy cheese and sour beer did their work. The foul air thickened. Let up on deck each day to stretch their legs, the colonists blinked in the pale sunshine, shivered in the cold and returned to their den, the stench the worse and the moans of the sick more piteous. One night, two boys escaped and word got out that there was plague aboard the *Bonaventure*. The harbourmaster told Yarwood to get his cargo clear of the port, and with regret, he did so. By the time they sailed, the passengers had more space, for now there were only seventy of them. The rest would never see Virginia, or any other land.

The ship plunged and yawed its way into the channel and south-west for the Canaries and warmer seas. Bess found the motion of the ship familiar and after the first day not disagreeable. She comforted those around her. There were children of eleven and twelve and some waifs who did not know their ages. Some, like Bess, were uncertain of their names.

She cradled the weakest children in her arms when they could not sleep and brought them water and made them laugh with tales of her companions on the road. That much she knew of herself.

'Thou'rt more like a maid than a man in thy ways, Ben,' said one farm lad, as she wiped the smeared face of a sick child with a rag.

She flashed him a glance. 'It's all one for us, maid or man, in this charnel house.'

'Pray God, 'twill soon be over and we land in Virginia,' said the lad.

'Dost think to be any better off?' asked another miserably.

'Speak for thyself,' came the reply, 'I've a paper sealed by the Company, that says after seven years I'm to have my freedom and two acres of prime land.'

'Aye, once thy premium and the voyage is paid,' said another. 'I've heard of those that had to serve another term, when the crops failed.'

'Then why didst thou embark?' asked the first lad.

'It came to my mind, I'd as lief starve in a new land as the old. But what of thee, Ben?'

'I was not asked. The Sheriff's man engaged on my behalf.'

'But hast thou no indenture, Ben?'

'Nay, I was sealed with a scratch from a soldier's blade.'

'Then thou'll serve for life.'

Bess's eyes flashed.

'It's not in my mind to serve any man so long.'

'What wilt do, leap overboard and seek thy brother in Darien?'

Bess shrugged off their laughter. 'I'd liefer go seek my brother, than weep for my mother like some I've heard.'

'Aye, but what of thy mother? Did she rock thee as thou dost rock that child?'

'My mother died 'ere I was born,' said Bess, then stopped in wonder. In her mind she suddenly saw a crowd of people on horseback, a blue sky, a bird on the wing, smelt the scent of heather, heard the splash of water.

'Ben, what dost dream on?'

'Nought, nought.'

When the ship reached calmer water, the passengers were

let up on deck. They awkwardly walked the tilting boards as the ship drove on under a blue sky with scudding white clouds. Some of the crew and the strongest of passengers were set with burning broom and vinegar to disinfect the quarters. The roll-call was now sixty-five. Yarwood was anxious. He opened his store and brought out extra rations.

The ship drove before the wind and the youngsters began to recover their spirits. When a mountain peak appeared on the horizon and the sailors cried 'Guadeloupe', some cheered. The bosun shook his head.

'Nay, we've a few leagues to go yet, south of Hispaniola and Jamaica, 'cross the Bay of Mexico and through the Florida Passage.'

'But shall we pass no islands?' said Bess anxiously.

'That we might. There are islands south of the Tortugas. But there be nought but hogs and wild cattle and Cimaroons and buccaneers.'

'Cimaroons I know,' said Bess. 'But what are those others?'

'Buccaneers, lad, are what we call cow killers. They hunt the beasts, dry the meat and sell it to all comers, English, Dutch, French, trader or privateer. They are desperate rogues, for when they tire of cattle they catch men and flay them.'

'What men do they hunt?'

'Spaniards for the most part. Buccaneers are godless knaves, but all good Protestants,' and the bosun laughed and went his way.

That night Bess spoke to her friends.

'I've a plan. We'll beg the skipper let us land on an island shore. The ship needs fresh water and we can wash our clothes and swim.'

The younger ones were excited, but an older lad was doubtful.

'He'll say nay. He's a hard man is Yarwood.'

And the lad was right. Next morning, when they were allowed on deck, Bess saw a grey shadow on the northern horizon, marking another island. She went to the Captain and drew off her tattered cap.

'What's your pleasure, Master Moore?' said Yarwood.

Bess told him. The mockery vanished. 'What, and lose my guests?'

'Nay, who'd run away?' said Bess.

'I know of a few, one not least,' retorted Yarwood. 'Nay, that can wait. Virginia's not far and when you're there, there's be time enough for washing,' he chuckled.

'Get them below,' he called to the bosun, and the sailors hustled them down.

The day wore on, the sun climbed the sky and the heat between decks began to grow. The lads and girls began to complain and the smaller ones to weep.

'Nay, 'tis past all reason, why should we not go ashore for an hour?' said one lad.

'True, why should we not?' said others.

'I have a plan,' said Bess.

They looked at her.

'Let one of us mount the ladder and beat on the door. And cry out that someone has died.'

'Aye, what then?'

'They'll send down two men to bear the corpse away.'

'Then . . .'

'Then we'll hold them by force till Yarwood lets us ashore.'

'Aye, let's do it,' they shouted.

One lad clambered up the ladder, beat on the door and shouted.

'A death. A death. Come bear them away. It grows foul here.'

The door was roughly flung open and the lad pushed aside as two sailors climbed down.

'Where's your dead?'

'Over here in the corner.'

'Here?'

'Nay, farther over.'

'Now,' called Bess and a dozen leapt on each man, grappling and kicking.

'Hold them. Strike them not,' yelled Bess. The two sailors lay prone, pinned down by the weight of their attackers.

'Now, keep them quiet, and wait,' she commanded.

But one of the sailors wriggled his head free and began to bawl.

'Save us. They'll murder us.'

The bosun's head showed in the companion way opening.

'What's amiss down there?'

Bess shouted: 'We have two bodies down here, Master Bosun. And they'll not come up till we have leave to go on shore.'

' 'Tis thee, Ben, thou knave,' swore the bosun and began to climb down.

'Watch thyself,' called Bess. 'We are three score. Wilt join thy shipmates?'

The bosun drew back.

'We'll not harm them. But leave us go on shore an hour and we shall set them free.'

The bosun disappeared. In his place stood Yarwood.

'Perchance I was a little hard, Ben lad.' He looked to landward. 'Why, we're but a cannon shot from shore, see. Do but come up all of ye. Come up.'

'Stay a moment,' said Bess.

But the others paid no heed. They rushed for the ladder and crowded on deck, capering and yelling. Bess was swept to one side. In the rush went those who were holding the sailors.

'Now,' yelled Yarwood down the hatch. 'Seize me that young knave.'

The two sailors, now freed, sprang up and grabbed Bess, twisted her arms behind her back, and bundled her up the ladder. The lads and girls were crowded towards the after deck, guarded by sailors with pike and cutlass. Yarwood himself held a pistol.

The ship, drawn on only by its foresail, lay close in to the island – Bess could see an open beach and the white foam of waves. Beyond that the green of deep forest and farther off the crown of a hill.

'No leg-stretching for thee, Ben Moore,' said Yarwood, 'but a back-warming. To the mainmast with him and let's see the colour of his skin.'

As the two sailors dragged Bess towards the mast she twisted in their arms, struck down like a snake and bit the nearest fingers. With a curse the man let go. She jerked free and ran into the crowd. They parted to let her through and the sailors, who ran after her, tripped over outstretched legs. Bess leapt to the rail, hauled herself up by the ratlines and as her pursuers pushed through the excited crowd, pushed herself off from the side of the ship.

To yells and oaths, she fell into the water. Surfacing, she struck out for land, swimming with all her strength. As she rolled in her stroke she looked back. The ship sailed on. She swam farther, looked back again. No boat was being lowered. Yarwood had decided it was good riddance.

'Amen,' said Bess, floating on her back to get back her breath. She saw the mainsail creep up the mast. They were leaving her.

An hour passed as Bess swam and floated in the water.

Exhausted, she crawled through the waves on to the shore, dragged herself several paces up the sloping beach away from the water, and there sank down.

Chapter thirteen

'Hey.'

Something dug into Bess's ribs. She rolled over, but the nudge came again, more sharply.

'Hey, amigo.'

Bess opened her eyes. She saw, a foot away from her nose, a black scarred face with strong white teeth.

'T'viens du bateau, huh?'

Another voice from her left. Behind the black man was another with pale blue eyes and bristling blond hair.

'Waar kom jy van daan?'

Bess's head swung round to the right. This time the speaker had a red pimply face and hair to match the fiery skin.

She understood not a word, but the faces grinned. She shook her head.

'Ingles, ha?' The black man spoke. 'You – English?'

Bess nodded.

'I leapt from the ship,' she pointed out to sea.

'Ship – gone.' The black man took her arm and pulled her up. She noted their dress; half-cured hides, long curved knives in their belts, and the muskets at their backs.

'Who are you?' she asked.

The black man tapped his chest – 'Manuel'. He pointed to the blond man 'Henri', and to the red-haired man 'Hans'. Bess pointed to herself – 'Ben'.

Manuel beckoned. The others walked swiftly over the beach and into the forest. They made their way lightly in long strides, turning, leaping over fallen logs, skirting bushes, while Bess found it hard to keep up with them. Then the ground swept upward and they broke out of the woods on to a small headland. Below lay a cove with a narrow beach. Beyond the treeline were small shelters of branches and a smouldering fire, from which came a smell of cooking meat that brought pain to Bess's stomach.

'Pig.' Hans smacked his lips as all sat down on logs round the fire. Bess took the smoking meat offered her on a bark plate and tore it with her teeth. She had not tasted meat since that night in the ruined church when she fed full on stolen mutton.

'Ship – where bound?' asked Manuel.

'Virginia.'

'Why you swim?'

Bess pointed to her back and made beating movements.

Manuel nodded and pointed to his own back.

'Art thou a Cimaroon?' she asked.

He pointed to the forest.

'Cimaroons – two leagues. Here buccaneer – cow killer.'

The meal over, they took her to a couch of branches and grass in the shade of the rocks.

'Sleep,' said Manuel.

Bess woke when it was night. She heard quiet breathing and saw two figures stretched out by the embers of the fire. A third figure silhouetted against the skyline was on watch.

Next day the three men went to the woods and bid her follow. In a clearing were three grazing horses, low slung, shaggy beasts, but wild and powerful. They mounted and rode off slowly, leaving her to follow on foot. An hour's march brought them to open grassland, where distant movement told Bess that herds were grazing.

Hans and Henri circled round stealthily and cut out several of the long-horned cattle, driving them down towards Manuel, who swung his horse across the path of the now frightened steers. Bess watched, amazed at the speed with which the beasts were lassoed, speared with cruel long lances and brought down. With barely a pause the carcasses were skinned and cut up. By the time the sun had reached full height, the party was on its way back to shore, walking now, the horses laden with meat and hides.

That night, Manuel woke Bess from her couch and led her to the headland, thrust a musket in her hand and said, 'You watch.'

Near dawn she drifted off to sleep. She was woken by a cuff on the head from Henri. 'N'dor pas. You not sleep.'

When they went again to the clearing next day, Bess raced ahead of the others and leapt on to Manuel's horse, shouting to him, 'You walk!'

The others shouted with delight. Manuel grinned and whistled to his horse.

The beast jerked forward, leapt several paces and stopped abruptly, going back on his haunches. There was no saddle, no stirrup, nothing but a rope bridle. Bess grasped it, hung on desperately with clenched knees.

'I'll not walk,' she swore to herself.

Manuel whistled again. The horse sank on his knees, leaving Bess almost sitting on his head. She held fast and Henri and Hans shouted encouragement.

Again Manuel whistled in a higher key and the wild horse spun round like a top, snatching with its teeth at Bess's legs. Jerking to avoid his bite, she lost her grip and was thrown. Manuel hauled her up and cuffed her.

'You walk,' he said, leaping on to his horse.

The three, mounted, set off again laughing and talking to each other. Bess turned back to the camp. But Manuel, moving with smooth speed, snatched the rope coil from his belt and let it fly. Bess felt herself jerked from her feet as the loop circled her shoulders. Before she could stagger to her feet, she was dragged several yards through the bush. She felt her heart ready to burst with rage as she tramped behind them, arms pinned to her sides. When they reached the grassland, Manuel released her and again she watched the slaughter and butchery and again she tramped back to the camp. That night she slept heavily and without interruption.

Next day Bess thought it prudent to walk as bidden. She was told, by signs, to load up the carcasses and skins, and she did this skilfully enough for she had watched her companions carefully.

That night, Manuel roused her in the small hours. This time she did not sleep and Henri greeted her at dawn with a grin.

That day, Bess was fully aware why she had been welcomed so casually by these three men. They needed her as a fourth partner for the watch, and as a labourer to load their beasts.

'Well,' she thought, 'two sides to a bargain.' She let another day pass and on the second day at sundown, as they sat by the fire, she addressed them all simply.

'No horse. No watch,' she said.

For a moment they looked astonished. Then Hans and Henri laughed. Manuel picked up a rope's end and leapt over the fire. But Bess was quicker.

She raced down to the shore, skipped nimbly upon a rock and as Manuel reached her, dived quickly into the water. As she came up for air, she saw them still standing on the shore. She had guessed right: none of them could swim.

'Farewell,' she shouted. 'I'll seek better mates.'

'Wait,' yelled Manuel. 'You watch tonight. Tomorrow, horse.'

The promise was kept. Next day, Manuel bid her ride behind him and the four went to another part of the prairie, where the giant black man and his mates rounded up a small band of wild ponies and drove them past for her inspection. She chose a rangy piebald beast and the others, nodding their approval, lassoed him.

For the next few days, they stayed in camp, lounging by the fire and watching her efforts to break in her mount. It was no easy task, but she knew she must not give in. And in the end it was the piebald who yielded. From then on, she rode with them when they raided the herds. Manuel taught her to use lance and lasso, Hans taught her the art of stripping and butchery, and Henri trained her to use the musket.

She grew stronger, her muscles hardened, and her skin toughened and blackened. She hacked off her hair with a butchering knife as it grew, and soon enough with the passing of the months, came to look like the younger brother of her companions. She needed both foresight and cunning to conceal her secret identity from her companions, slipping aside from time to time to wash her body, clean her clothes and the worn cloth that bound in her breasts. Her lean figure, unlimited energy and fierce temper helped her disguise. The others looked on her with rough friendliness. Manuel never raised his hand against her again, but instead began to treat her with strange gentleness.

As she picked up the mixture of four languages her companions used, so she learned why they were always on their guard. They had formed part of a larger buccaneer band, led by a Frenchman, on an island some ten miles north. As this gang had turned more and more to raiding Spanish ships sailing out of Santo Domingo to the north-west, so had the cruelties of their leader increased. A Spanish expedition had taken its revenge, destroyed their hideout and the three had been lucky to escape to a new island. Here they lay low, exchanging cured meat and hides with passing Dutch ships for powder, blades and tobacco.

They neither talked of their own homelands nor questioned Bess about her past. There was an unspoken law that only the present counted; the past was the past, the future no man could know.

The Dutch ships which circled the islands and the shores of Terra Firma, picking an illegal living under the noses of the Spanish viceroys, aroused Bess's curiosity. 'Did they sail near the Darien shore?' she asked one skipper.

'I do not, but there's another vessel comes by here, that sails now and then to the salt pans down there. Ask of him.'

Manuel heard her talk to the captain and demanded to know the reason. When he heard Bess's tale of a lost brother on the shores of the Gulf of Darien, he frowned and said: 'Thou'lt not leave us.'

But there was a gentle note in his voice that struck to her heart.

Next day as they rode to the herds, Manuel rested his great hand lightly on her neck for a moment. Bess stirred uneasily, but did not ride on for fear of offending him. But that night, when he woke Bess to stand watch, Manuel stroked her cheek and kissed her gently on the lips. A strange feeling flowed through her, half pleasure, half fear. She slid away from him and walked to the headland.

She brooded on this strange turn of events for a full hour until the dawn began to show grey on the very edge of the sky. Then she made up her mind.

She stole back to the camp, took more shot for her musket, a pouch of dried meat, and while the others still slept she stole into the forest. For most of the morning she lay there, until the sound of her companion's voices calling 'Ben, Ben,' began to die away. In the afternoon, she came down to the shore and set off towards the other end of the island.

For a month she lived alone, hunting by day, hiding in a tree shelter at night, often moving on to a new place. Sometimes she heard far off the sound of her friends' muskets. She felt their loss keenly but did not dare return. Every few days she would come down to the shore and look out for ships.

Always it was empty, until the fifth week when she spied a sail from the north-east, on a course that would bring it past the island. As it came nearer she saw that it was indeed the Dutch salt ship. Swiftly she built a fire, loaded it with wet leaves and sent up a column of smoke.

As the ship kept on course, she loaded her musket and fired a shot.

The ship hove to and lowered a boat. Bess left the shelter of the woods and ran down to meet it as it drew in to the beach.

She was knee-deep in the waves shouting a welcome in broken Dutch, when she knew her error.

The ship was a Spanish prize. She turned to run back to land, but a blow from a sword hilt toppled her into the water.

Chapter fourteen

The tall man in elegant black with white lace at his throat stood out among the crowd that swarmed the quay at Santo Domingo. Spanish soldiers in rusty armour, traders and market women in brilliant clothes, black slaves stripped to the waist, pushed, cursed and joked. But the tall man with the hooked nose and keen brown eyes looked on all with quiet amusement. A port official tried in vain to catch his attention. As the ship came into harbour, its sails gently folding down, the official tried again.

'A fine prize, Senor.'

The man raised his eyebrows. 'You mean that this time you'll get the Dutch cargo free instead of sneaking down the coast to buy it behind the Viceroy's back?'

The port official, who knew that the Viceroy's secretary was bribed by the merchants and that the Viceroy took his share to turn a blind eye to contraband trade, did not reply. He was unsure about Don Santiago Alvaros, who had come so lately from Seville and yet seemed to know so much. No one, not even the staff at the palace knew what was his errand in the Audiencia of Santo Domingo. He came from a powerful family yet he had taken no office in the port, nor, as far as anyone knew, had he accepted anything from anyone, not even compliments.

The ship tied up at the quay. Soldiers began to push back the crowd and the official signalled to two slaves who brought forward a brazier with glowing charcoal, and iron rods.

'Not so close,' he snapped, 'I'm warm enough.'

Then he turned to Alvaros who had raised a hand.

'Senor?'

'The Dutch ship's officers will go under guard straight to the palace. The rest you can take.'

Slowly the captives from the prize ship began to climb up to the quay. At a sign from Alvaros two were taken aside and led away, though Alvaros himself still did not move.

One by one the manacled captives were led to the brazier, their shirts stripped from their backs, the branding rod with the glowing tip pressed swiftly to their chests and the victims hustled away almost before the cry of pain could rise to their lips.

As the last one was led up, the port official said, 'Wait. That's no Hollander. 'Tis a cow killer. The clothes and the stink tell all.'

As the captive's shirt, rotten with wear, ripped away, someone in the crowd shouted and pointed. The port official stared, the man with the branding iron hesitated. The man in black who had begun to move away, turned back.

'Madonna,' cried the official. ' 'Tis a counterfeit man, a maid dressed as a youth.'

As if suddenly aware of the indignity of standing half naked before the shouting, jesting crowd, the lean figure of the girl sprang into life. Moving with speed despite the gyves on ankles and wrists, she snatched up the branding iron and thrust it near the face of the port official. As the red heat breathed on his skin, the plump man collapsed on the quay.

'Ha,' shouted the girl in broken Spanish, 'a counterfeit man.'

The crowd roared. The slave snatched back the iron and his partner seized the girl again.

'Wait.'

They halted.

'Strike off the maid's irons. Quick,' commanded Don Alvaros.

When it was done, he beckoned to the girl. 'Come with me. But first put on your jacket. You may not walk in the streets with me like that.'

She stared at him, bewildered. 'Who are you?'

'That does not concern you. Come.'

Don Alvaros strode away, leaving the revived official gaping and protesting. The girl followed, rubbing her wrists where the manacles had chafed the skin. A wide street led through an avenue of tall palms and into a broad square. At one side, the imposing decorated front of a church, at the other the Viceroy's Palace. Don Alvaros walked across the square, then passing under the arches of an arcade below the palace, stepped through a small gate, waving the girl after him.

They were now in an enclosed garden. Don Alvaros watched the girl from the corner of his eye.

'She is befouled,' he thought, 'but beneath the filth she is fair and proud.'

He called a servant and said quietly. 'Take the maid – aye, 'tis a maid. Have her washed thoroughly and dressed – gown, petticoat, shawl and such other ornaments as suit what you discover beneath the dirt. Then bring her to my apartment.'

Upstairs in his own room, Don Alvaros took his cup of chocolate, lightly spiced, and sat by a window overlooking the bay. From time to time, he would write in a small notebook. An hour passed before the servant knocked on the door.

'Don Alvaros. The maid is ready.'

Alvaros turned and looked at the girl. The curly black hair had been lightly bound in, the shoulders covered with a fine lace shawl over a fine black and white-striped gown. The deep sunburn had a shade of peach in it, that put him in mind of Creole girls. But this girl was no Creole.

'There's much of interest here,' he thought, and at once the prospect of his stay in Santo Domingo with its conniving merchants, its ruffianly officers and corrupt half-nobility, became attractive to him.

Who was she? First he would try to guess. He pointed to the

chair on the other side of the window, told her to be seated while he paced about the room.

'You are no Hollander,' he said suddenly.

'Why should I tell you ought?' she replied calmly.

He listened, trying to detect the accent. 'Why should you not? I saved you from the galleys.'

'For what?'

'That I do not yet know myself. But I love mystery. I live by it. You are a mystery. You are a lady, you are no drab or camp-follower. Yet you dwelt among the cow-killers.'

She shrugged.

'You are not afraid of what will happen if you displease me?'

'Senor . . .'

'Santiago Alvaros is my name.'

'Senor Alvaros,' she spoke slowly, 'I have lived through much in twelve months. You may still be able to surprise me, but frighten me, no.'

'Bravo,' he said, clapping his hands. Now he had the accent.

'What is your name?' he shouted in English.

The girl's eyes clouded. His voice sounded strange.

'Ben Moore, sir.'

'Ben Moore. That is your alias, your cloak as a man. But you are English, and I shall not call you Ben, it offends me.'

'B-Bess,' she said suddenly. Her shoulders relaxed.

'Elizabeth. After your late and noble Queen.'

'How so?' the question jerked from her.

'Elizabeth the Queen of England is no more. She died last spring. In her place reigns James of Scotland. Your new King has proclaimed that he was never at war with Spain. So our kingdoms are at peace.'

'And so?'

'And so, we have no right to hold an English lady – if such you are – against her will.'

'Ha.'

'What is your other name, Elizabeth?'

Her shoulders tensed.

'I – I know not.'

Alvaros sat down at the table again.

'Mystery within mystery. See, Mistress No-one. I, Don Alvaros, am in this city against my will.'

'Why so?'

'That is my mystery. You are here against your will. Let us pass the slow hours away in solving your mystery.'

'What then?'

'If you are a high-born lady I will pay court to you.'

'Is that honourable, Catholic to Protestant?'

'If our realms are at peace, who knows, these barriers to true friendship may fall.'

'And, if our realms go to war again?'

'Then you shall be my hostage – surety against the future.'

'You are a prudent man, Don Alvaros.'

'And you a most shrewd lady.'

He rose and called his servant. 'The lady will eat in my chamber. You will find her a maid. She shall stay in the bed chamber above.'

He turned to Bess. 'Until tomorrow at this hour. Eat well, rest well, Elizabeth No-One.'

Bess ate and drank at the small table. She marvelled at the delicate taste of it all. When she had finished, a tall black maid led her to the room above, and helped her to undress, then gave her a white shift.

'Judith,' said Bess. The name rose like a fish to the surface of her mind, then sank again. The maid stared.

Bess put a hand to her eyes. The maid helped her to the bed, then drew a fine white net over it. Bess sank into the scented sheets and into sleep almost in the same moment. Nor did she wake until next morning when the same maid drew back the net around the bed.

A narrow cup steamed on the table nearby.

'What's that?'

'Chocolate, lady.'

Bess tasted it. ' 'Tis rare.'

'Nay, lady. 'Tis common.'

Both laughed. The maid brought her a bowl with water and fresh clothes. The black and white dress had gone. The maid helped her dress, this time in scarlet and gold, with a flower for her hair, and held the glass for Bess to see.

'Farewell, Ben Moore,' she told her reflection.

Downstairs Don Alvaros waited. On his table were dishes, egg, fish, small fowl. They ate quietly, looking out on the busy port. The air was still and already warm.

Alvaros called for his carriage and they drove slowly from the city and into the nearby hills. Near noon they rested from the heat at an inn among the trees, and Don Alvaros questioned her closely, though gently, but could not break down the barrier of her memory.

But his quiet manner and soft voice calmed her. His attention flattered. It was a way of men with women that she had not known before.

That evening he entertained guests in his house and had Bess sit beside him. The guests, merchants and officers she could see, were trying to sound out Don Alvaros and he them. She was being used, she guessed, as a decoy, to throw them off the scent.

Her poor Spanish would not let her follow the conversations, but she heard the words, *flota, armada, avisos, gallizebras, armadas de barlovento,* and knew they talked of the Spanish treasure fleets. She guessed the other men were suspicious, even afraid of Alvaros.

She could tell he was a man of power, some power that seemed to stem from Spain itself and not from the Viceroy. She wondered if his curiosity about her was simply idle, or whether he was serious when he spoke of her as a 'surety' for the future. Why should he fear the future? And would he use her in that way, if it served his purpose? He treated her well, giving her the best of food, of clothes, and other attentions.

But he would allow no one, other than his servants, to speak to her, unless he were there. And he would not allow her to leave the apartment unless he were with her. She was treated as a lady – and as a prisoner.

As weeks slipped by this irked her more and more. If she were English he had no right to detain her. Clearly though, he'd no intention of sending her home. She had no urgent wish to go, she knew. To what or whom would she return? She had not submitted to be shipped on Yarwood's hulk, nor risked her life among the buccaneers, to return home yet. She had another goal.

Often as she talked to Alvaros she was tempted to tell him of her brother. Time and again, caution told her not to.

How long this might have gone on she could not say, but one day Alvaros came back from a meeting with the Viceroy with news that filled her with wild excitement.

'I must leave you, Elizabeth.'

Her heart seemed to miss a beat.

'Why?'

'I must take ship to Porto Bello.'

'Porto Bello?'

'Aye.'

'In Darien?'

Without thinking, she said, 'Then I'll go with you.'

Chapter fifteen

He looked astonished, then suddenly smiled.

'Woman of mysteries,' then, 'It may not be. My mission is a matter of weight. I may not be accompanied by a lady.'

'Then let me go as thy manservant.'

He stared.

'Hast thou not seen me play the man?'

'Right handily.' He paced the room, in thought, then: 'Why not? Santo Domingo is glad to see me go and cares not, Porto Bello fears me but knows me not. We are almost of a height. I'll have clothes sent to thy room. Dress without thy maid and join me in my chamber at dawn. But I'd ask one thing of thee.'

'What's that?'

'Take one gown in thy luggage.'

He reached out and pressed her hand. 'I will thank God I found thee here.'

She smiled. 'And I – God knows.'

The ship sailed soon after dawn, with Bess and Alvaros aboard. Bess had a small cubby-hole of a cabin next to his, and when they walked on deck, she paced a step behind him and said nothing. Her hair covered in a velvet cap, she looked a model servant.

But when the ship was in open sea, Alvaros sent for food and wine and they went into his cabin.

'Close and bolt the door,' he said, 'and put the shutter over the ports while I light candles.'

'What's afoot?'

'Why, Bess No-one. Thou and I must speak frankly with one another.'

'Who's to begin?'

'Thou, I fear. I must know who thou art. Art thou sent to spy on me?'

'I?' gasped Bess.

He went on: 'Why art thou so mad to come with me to Porto Bello? Come – the truth.'

'Can I trust thee?'

'If thou tell me the truth – with thy life.'

'Then, I'll tell thee. Somewhere in Darien I believe I have a brother.'

'What's his name?'

'Matthew.'

'Only Matthew?'

Bess burst out: 'If I knew my own name, I'd know his.' Her anger reassured Alvaros. He drank deeply.

'Bess, thy name is locked in thy heart. So is mine.'

'But thou art Santiago Alvaros.'

'That's my adopted name. Alvaros was as a father to me. But my name is other. Even to thee I'll not reveal it. But my family are Jews. Now Jews in Spain are made Christians, baptized by fire. My father could not make the leap and so the flames consumed him. I cherish life. So outwardly I'm Christian, inwardly a Jew. I live a secret. Secrets are my life. I have been the King of Spain's spy in lands abroad. Their tongues I speak as my own. Now, for my sins, I spy on Spaniards.'

'How so?'

'Each year, the wealth of our King's possessions is sent down to Porto Bello and to Vera Cruz in Mexico. Thence sail the ships to bear home – gold, silver, spices. Fast warships convoy them over the sea, safe from privateers. These days only Spaniards may steal from his Majesty.'

'And do they?'

'They do. And Don Alvaros goes prying and spying to discover what their secrets are.'

'But why? What dost thou owe the King of Spain?'

'Part of me hungers after secrets and discoveries, part of me burns with contempt for these gross fools and their scrabbling after money . . .'

He rose from the table.

'I'm tired of talking. Let's walk on deck.'

Day after day the ship sailed on, edging south, flying west. Each day, Don Alvaros and Bess walked, dined and talked. She learnt more of his life, but her own remained behind its curtain and none of Alvaros's questions found their mark.

Save once, he spoke of London. 'Troynovant, New Troy, they call it,' he smiled, 'and others know it as a huge cesspit where great and small labour to enrich themselves.'

'And do they not so in Spain?'

'Nay, not like that. The small folk labour but they are not enriched. The great enrich themselves, but labour not. In your tongue, work stands next to godliness, in our tongue, next to dishonour. Our nobles hold it in contempt. And while New Spain's rivers flow with gold, they will not change. The time's not far off when Spaniards will lose this empire. English and Dutch will take their place. Our hand is feeble. The glory departs.'

'What other places hast thou known in England?'

He thought for a while.

'Aye, there was one where my life was in peril. I was to discover how large were its fortifications and how many cannon.'

'What didst thou find?'

'The fortifications were half finished and the guns were borrowed, the merchants squabbled over who should pay the cost, and the warships that destroyed the Great Armada rotted at their moorings.'

'Where was it?'

'Why, Plymouth, in Devon.'

Plymouth – Bess saw in clear sunlight a boat under full sail, that breasted the waves, an old man in woollen cap at the tiller, a barrel-chested boy in the prow, and she heard a girl's voice say:

'Nay, to the World's End.'

Then the black curtain fell. She saw Alvaros stare at her. He gripped her wrist. 'Thou art from Plymouth. Thou art, Bess . . . Come speak, Bess . . .'

She burst into tears. He dropped his hand.

'Your pardon.'

Outside men ran on deck. Voices shouted.

'Tierra, tierra.'

'We come to Porto Bello,' said Alvaros.

They stayed two weeks in the port crowded with people from all parts of the Empire waiting the arrival of the fleet. Don Alvaros was engaged in long discussions with officials, and he came back to the lodging looking grim and tired.

'As I press on their heels, so it grows more perilous. I must set forth again.'

'Whither now?'

'We take ship to Nombre de Dios. Thence by mule to a river mouth, and by barge up river. So to Venta Cruz and down trail by mule to Panama.'

'Why this journey?'

'We follow our trail back along the route the silver takes. Somewhere along that trail I shall discover the hole in the sack through which the King of Spain's treasure pours.'

'When do we start?'

'By morning light.'

They stayed at an inn in Nombre de Dios while Alvaros arranged for an escort to ride with them to the river. While they waited the inn-keeper told them stories of the past. Seven years before, he had seen the fleet of Drake and Hawkins on their last fatal voyage.

'They came to plunder, but there was nought to be had.

All we might offer them was the plague, and of that they had plenty of their own.'

'What of Cimaroons?' asked Bess.

'When I was younger those devils ranged within our streets and ravaged our harbour. But now there's nought to hate here, nought to fear. Why in those days, they camped not seven leagues from these walls. Now they're gone farther beyond the Chagres and the road to Venta Cruz.'

He grew silent. Alvaros gave him money and his memory stirred again.

'They marched in three columns, like the wind. Our soldiers never knew from whence the next blow might fall. And I'll tell you something passing strange. I heard a soldier who fought them and lived to tell the tale, say that before them marched a warrior who sang.'

'Sang?'

'Aye. He was called in their tongue, "The Singer".'

'What did he sing?'

'I know not. But they say he did sing in the English tongue.'

'English?'

'Aye, 'twas passing strange.'

Next day the escort arrived, a sorry bunch of men in stained armour and threadbare uniform, some twenty in number. Alvaros called the alcade and demanded an explanation. But that gentleman looked sly and excused himself. Times were hard.

'May the mules be in better shape than the men,' muttered Alvaros.

They were, though the difference was slight and the journey along narrow trails through heavy forest along the coastline was slow.

On the second day's march some fifteen miles from Nombre de Dios, Bess asked the escort captain if he knew of an old Cimaroon town. He nodded.

'It lies westward, a league, no more, by the sea.'

Bess turned to Alvaros.

'Can we go there?' she begged.

He nodded and gave orders. The escort captain obeyed reluctantly, but one hour later the mule train turned off to the west and headed down to the coast. Another hour's journey brought them there and the captain pointed down the wooded slopes to a place above the sea. He refused to go farther.

'Wait there, then,' ordered Alvaros. Bess and he rode on down towards the sea and soon left the forest to come out on to a level headland which had been cleared of trees. There was the outline of a village, a double line of huts, roofless and broken down, a square trampled so hard that the grass had not yet grown. Within that square was a blackened area where fires had been built.

'Bess,' called Alvaros, 'come here.'

She found him by the ruins of a single small hut.

He pointed. Above the broken threshold crooked and broken, but still fixed to the doorpost, was a wooden cross.

'See here.'

Alvaros was on his knees before two moss-covered mounds nearby. Bess knelt down beside him and taking the knife he offered her began to cut away the moss. Soon stone appeared and then lower down, crude lettering. She scratched with more care.

'J-o-h-n, the grave of an Englishman,' said Bess. 'G-a-l, nay, I can read no more.'

'What of the other?' said Alvaros.

'Not so old. The moss is less thick.'

She scraped again. 'There are strange letters K-u-l, nay that means nought. Now see here – lower down – M-a-t-t,' she gasped, 'Matthew.' She felt the pain rise in her heart, well into her throat. Alvaros took the knife and went on scraping.

He spelt out 'M-o-r-t-e-n, Morten.'

As tears spilled down Bess's cheeks, the light broke through and the black curtain in her mind burst apart.

'I am Bess Morten and my brother Matthew is dead.'

Her head dropped on her hands. Alvaros knelt beside her and began to pray. Bess joined him, 'Father in heaven . . .'

Behind them the bushes rustled. Alvaros leapt to his feet, sword drawn. Bess faced south, Alvaros's knife in hand.

'There was someone there. Bess, we must go back, swiftly. Later when we make camp, we'll talk. God's mercy took thy brother but he has restored thee to thyself.'

They ran to the mules that grazed beneath the trees and set them climbing up the slope. Through Bess's mind flowed memories and pictures like a flood unloosed when a dyke is broken – her father dying, Dickon's drunken rage, Lady Ferrers's cold contempt. Now she would never know her brother as he was, but only as they saw him, like a face in a crooked glass.

Alvaros reached the party on the trail before her. She saw the soldiers waiting on the main track, and urged her mule up the last score of yards. Alvaros was already dismounted, sword in hand.

'Treachery,' he shouted. 'Bess, fly for thy life.'

To her horror, from behind the soldiers a man she had not seen, an officer on a black horse, thrust forward. In his hand was a pistol. He fired and Alvaros dropped to the ground.

The soldiers closed round her, seized the reins of her mount and she was dragged at a clumsy gallop along the trail behind them.

Chapter sixteen

The trail now left the forest and ran through open country with waist-high grass. After several miles in dust and heat with the sun at its height, a halt was called and the party sheltered under a solitary tree.

Her captor eyed Bess.

'So you are Alvaros's Englishwoman?'

'And you are his assassin.'

'His executioner and your jailer.'

'Where are you taking me?'

'To Guatemala City. The visitor-general of the Inquisition is there and has many questions to ask you before you burn.'

'Burn?'

'As a witch who caused Alvaros to betray his King and realm.'

'Then you should hang as a traitor and murderer. Alvaros betrayed none but thieves.'

He was amused.

'But, say I did not kill him. Say we found him dead by the trail and you rifling the corpse?'

'What of your soul and those of your soldiers?'

'The visitor-general will see to them.'

Bess spoke coldly. 'You do not believe I am a spy. You and the men you serve have seen your chance to destroy Alvaros, through me. Your silence answers me. Poor Alvaros, if he'd not saved my life, he'd be alive today.'

'You think so? You are wrong. A man like Alvaros is doomed. And you are doomed along with him.'

The sergeant of the escort spoke anxiously: 'Captain. We must make haste. There's more forest between here and the river. We dare not be benighted there.'

The officer laughed: 'What do you fear, man? The witch?'

The soldier crossed himself. 'Captain. Our men heard something move beside us near the trail. They fear the Cimarrones.'

'Fools, knaves,' said the Captain. 'The Cimarrones are gone beyond the river. You fear your own shadows. Ride on.'

Reluctantly the men remounted and rode on. The dark shape of the forest drew nearer and as the party passed into the green gloom beneath the trees, men and mounts began to bunch together.

'Forward and make haste.' The first riders broke into a trot then halted.

'Who dares halt?' yelled the captain galloping from the rear.

'Who dares go on?' shouted Bess mockingly.

'Listen, Captain,' the soldier's voice shook.

'I hear nothing but the chattering of your cowardly teeth.'

'No, hear now,' the man insisted.

'It is the Singer,' whispered an old soldier and crossed himself.

From the forest before them came the sound of singing, distant and melancholy. The voice floated on the still forest air with strange beauty. Bess suddenly made out the words.

'Did not the Lord promise us?'

From both sides of the track came the thrilling chant:

'The Lord promised.'

Hearts chilled with fear, the soldiers heard again the solitary voice.

'Land in Canaan.'

And the deep-throated chorus:

'Canaan land.'

One soldier found his voice.

'We are lost. Save yourselves.'

He turned his mount and instantly the column broke in confusion, horses and mules trampling one another.

A voice called from nearby, clearly, in English.

'Throw thyself down.'

As Bess threw herself from her mule she heard the deadly hiss of arrows and the shrieks of men in agony. Near her a dying rider fell from his plunging horse. The lashing hooves struck her head a glancing blow and she lost consciousness.

She found her senses for a brief moment to feel herself carried swiftly along, the trees above her a green blur. Then she fainted again.

When her eyes opened, she was on a brushwood bed. Above her a roof of leaves; farther off, huts, trees, a river and the distant sky. A woman with a clay pitcher bent down and offered her a drink, then left as two men appeared. They squatted on their heels a yard away from her head and regarded her. They were not young. One's hair was white, the other's iron-grey and crisply curled.

The grey-haired man was black, his powerful face marked by a branching scar that gave his features the look of Satan. But the teeth gleamed in a smile.

The other man, his face lined and burned deep brown by the sun, was marked by a smaller scar at the side of his face. Bess stared at the face which smiled at her. A hand brushed the hair from her eyes. She seized it and held it to her cheek.

'Thou art my brother, whom I thought dead. Thou art Matthew.'

' 'Tis so. And thou art Bess, my sister.'

'How didst thou know?'

'We had word of a Spanish column from Nombre de Dios. We learnt that an Englishwoman travelled with it. And we saw you come to our old town.'

'But, the stone in the ground.'

'It marks the burying place of Kulokela, my dear wife. Sister to Ba-umba, chief of the Talusi, my friend.'

'And thine,' said the black man to Bess.

'Whose was the other grave?' asked Bess.

'That of John Galton, my friend.'

'He that they said you slew?'

'He that I slew.'

'Nay,' said the black man. 'Galton died by mischance, when Matthew gave my people their freedom.'

'He did loose the cargo,' said Bess, half to herself.

'Aye,' said Ba-umba. 'That he did. He did free the Talusi, and here,' he pointed to the huts around, 'they live today.'

'Matthew is our brother, too, and for his sake we sent our men below the river to set you free. Our men do not lightly cross the river. Below that river we have known only battles.'

There was something hidden in Ba-umba's tone but what it was Bess could not say.

Matthew saw her frown and laid his hand on her forehead. 'We will leave thee now, sister. Sleep, and tomorrow we shall be merry together.'

Next morning Bess was awakened by the sun shining into her shelter. And with the sun, came Matthew. Behind him trailed a crowd of children, naked, dark and grinning.

'Thy children, brother?'

'Children of the flesh have I none. Kulokela, my dear wife, died of the plague and I have stayed single for her sake. But as I am of this people I have many children.'

Turning he clapped his hands and told them go and play. They ran a few yards off and stood watching Bess.

'If thou wilt change thy clothes, Bess, we have thy mule and saddle bags.'

Bess sat up and studied her crumpled shirt and breeches. She looked across the square at the women passing by, noted the light, knee-length shifts they wore.

'The women's dress here is light and comely.'

'If thou'rt not wedded to thy shirt and breeches.'

'Nay, with me 'tis no religion, but as sorteth with me best.'

'Sister, come to my hut, and let us eat and talk.'

Matthew gave her goat's milk and cheese and manioc bread to eat and then they strolled down through tall trees to the sea. From the wide beach that swept in a great circle to high headlands on either side, she could see canoes putting out to sea.

'They go fishing or hunt for turtle eggs. The sea, the land have all we need,' said Matthew.

Bess breathed the air and looked about her.

' 'Tis paradise.'

' 'Tis true, but no eternal life.'

'And no angel with a sword to drive us out.'

'Bess, thou canst stay so long it pleases thee. And – may it be long. Think now. Two days ago, I was alone. And now I have a sister. Wilt stay?'

She hesitated. Wherever she went, someone sought to keep her, some by force, some by gentler ties.

Matthew read her thoughts. 'I'm a selfish knave. 'Twas ever my weakness. See Bess,' he pointed out to sea. 'Ten leagues off lies an island, even fairer than our land here. The Spaniards call it Maravila – Marvel. They come not there these days, but Dutch ships pass by, salt ships and others, English, French rovers. When thou wilt home to Plymouth, say the word, and we will see thee safe aboard a boat for home.'

Bess reddened at her own thoughts.

'I have not sought my brother on the Darien shore so long to go away again, so soon. But, Matthew, something tells me thy friend Ba-umba is not happy to have me here.'

He protested, ' 'Tis not so. Understand him. His one thought is to save his people. He led them from slavery as Moses did.'

'Aye, Spanish slavery.'

'Into which they were sold by Englishmen.'

'And freed by an Englishman.'

They paced the shore. Bess took flat stones and skimmed them over the milk-smooth water.

'Matthew?'

'Aye?'

'Didst thou slay thy friend?'

His voice was heavy. 'I did employ a trick to set Ba-umba's people free. In their flight he was slain.'

'Then thy intent was good.'

Matthew took her hand. 'See, Bess, I know not if my intent was good or bad. I let them go that others might not enrich themselves from slavery. But, if Susannah Combe had been my bride, if that black cargo had been dowry for her to wed me and not Charles Ferrers whom I hated, would I have done the deed?'

'Matthew. Give not thyself short weight.'

'Perchance,' said Matthew. 'But 'tis dead and gone these thirty years and more. And Bess, 'tis thirty years since I've seen Plymouth.'

'There's much to tell.'

'Then tell it slowly, for I have time enough.'

Bess's story began as they walked by the sea. In the evening as they sat together before Matthew's hut, his friends around them, she continued.

Sometimes Ba-umba was there, quietly listening. She saw his eyes on her, calm and friendly, but withdrawn. Each day, she told more of her story, pausing to let the memories return. Once when they walked upon the hills above the town and they were alone, she told him of their father's death.

'Ah, then. His soul's at rest,' said Matthew, 'I did hurt him grievously then, but did not know it.'

'What was it?'

'I did blame him that he took coin from others for his preaching and praying. Poor father, he had a weight of sin on him. He did believe that sin, gold-plated, shines in the eye of the Lord.'

'Nay, Matthew. That's unjust. Father was charitable. He gave to the poor.'

Matthew turned to face her.

'No man giveth to the poor. Some men give back what hath been taken from them. If it were not so, then were they never poor.'

'Are not the poor always with us?'

'Bess. I have seen in 50 years men run as in a race, and always after gold. Some win, others fall behind. Some sail into port with gold in their pocket, some die; the glitter in their eye is fever. I count the race well lost if I may have my life . . .'

'*Ubi omnes omnia pecuniis,*' murmured Bess.

'Aye, good Sir Thomas More had it right – where money rules, the Commonwealth doth wither.'

Bess looked out to sea. From the hill the island of Maravila rose distant and grey on the horizon.

'Sir Thomas did dream of a Utopia land where all life's ills might be cured.'

' 'Tis so, Bess.'

'And he did never find it?'

'Not this side of Jordan river. He said his marvellous land was Nowhere.'

'But is that so, Matthew? Is there nowhere folk may find their ease?'

He took her face between his hands and kissed her forehead. 'In a book a skipper gave me, I did read . . .

> *Rest after toil, port after stormy seas,*
> *Peace after war, do greatly please.*

'Ease is not found, but made, Bess.'

'Hast thou made thine?'

'Aye, and now I have seen thee I ask no more.'

Months passed, a golden circle of days, bounded each evening by thunder cloud, swift downpour and the freshening of the air.

Crops grew, were harvested, planted and harvested – twice in a season. Bess saw it with wonder. She said to Matthew: 'If all our poor wanderers might strike root here, they might find – might make their ease.'

He smiled and said nothing.

Bess swam, went out with the fishing canoes, sat with the crowds that sang round fires at sunset, watched the young men and women dancing, marvelled how they sought one another out in the light of the flames.

Matthew lent her from his small store of books, broken-backed, blotched with mildew, the gifts of passing skippers. She read in them and then demanded of Matthew why he neither preached nor prayed.

'I had a little chapel and did teach the gospel. Some slaves who fled the plantations came to hear the word, and, after our fashion, began to dispute. After disputes came blows. Old Akenoro did forbid it and I ceased.'

'Who is Old Akenoro?'

'Ba-umba's father. His son bears the same name – a great one. The lad is worthy of it.'

'I have not seen him.'

'No, he's away in distant parts on a great errand for his father.'

'What's that?'

'Ba-umba seeks to draw together all wandering Cimaroon bands into a Confederacy and retreat with them into a place deep in the forest – a famous spot, by a great lake. No Spaniard comes near.'

'When will this be?'

'In years. Ba-umba thinks he will not live to see it. Akenoro will lead them there.'

'Wilt thou go too?'

'Nay, I'll stay here alive or dead. I'll not move again. But, Bess, I fear that thou dost begin to long after home.'

' 'Tis strange, Matthew. I do and I do not.' She thought a while. 'Ben Moore would lie here in the sun. Bess Morten would go back to Plymouth, to claim what men deny her – to rule her fortune and her fate.'

'But is thy fortune thy fate, Bess? Canst thou not be without it?'

She smiled wryly, 'I'll not be denied.'

He looked at her strangely, 'Aye, thou'lt go back, like it or not, understand it or not. So I did once myself.'

Next day, Bess heard from a hunter that there were herds of wild cattle and horses near the river They must have broken free from some Spanish estancia and swum across the river when the water was low.

Bess leapt to her feet : 'Canst guide me there?'

The young man nodded. Matthew grinned.

'See, Matthew, I'd have rope, a lance, a knife with a keen blade. Canst get me these?'

He smiled again. 'It can be done.'

Before the day was half over, Bess had left the village with a hunting party. They were away three days and returned on the fourth, leading half a dozen wild horses, and carrying loads of freshly killed meat.

That night around the fire, with Matthew's aid, Bess told the young hunters that she would teach them to ride the wild ponies.

'The Talusi have never gone on horseback,' said Matthew.

'Then they shall begin. For it was on horseback the Dons conquered this land.'

The young hunters, when they heard her words, nodded vigorously. Then they gestured to one another and laughed.

'What do they say?' asked Bess.

Matthew answered : 'They dispute, whether a man would be happy to have thee to wife, or not.'

'Indeed?'

'Aye. Some say "yea, for then he might live in idleness," and others, "nay, for he would be outfaced."'

'Let them have no fear. I've no plans to wed, but only to break horses.'

The breaking-in of the wild horses took most of the summer, and teaching the young hunters to ride them took the rest. But before they could return to the herds, the rains began, the forest streams rose above their banks and the hunt had to be abandoned.

When the rains stopped and the water courses began to dry, the hunters on horseback roamed the country north of the river. The herds had increased, and this time they brought back both mares and foals. That summer the town was supplied with meat and hides for curing. Bess and her hunters began to talk of a great drive to shift the herds farther north and bring them closer to the town.

But one day as she went to get ready her horse, she found the town in great excitement. People were leaving their homes and rushing down to the sea. Even the oldest went, being helped or carried. As they hurried to the shore, the people spoke one name to one another.

Bess found Matthew about to leave his hut.

'Aye, 'tis Akenoro who returns,' he said.

Chapter seventeen

Matthew and Bess stood amid the crowds on the beach, watching as two long double canoes, great triangular sails furling, slowly drew into shore. As they grounded, men leapt out to drag them up the shore. Families crowded round weeping and shouting their delight.

Three men, young and tall, stepped more slowly from the canoes and advanced up the shelving sand.

'First comes Akenoro and behind him his younger brothers,' said Matthew.

The crowd made way and Ba-umba came to greet them. Bess saw the son was taller than the father, though less powerfully built.

'A handsome lad and a good one,' whispered Matthew.

Now Ba-umba, Akenoro at his side, walked slowly past them. The young man saw Matthew and broke away with a delighted shout of 'Uncle' and seized the older man by the shoulders.

'A good journey, Akenoro?'

'A good journey. And who is this?'

'My sister, Bess.'

Their eyes met. He looked down first, but smiled.

'This is a secret, Uncle. You had no sisters.'

'I did not know I had, but I am glad.'

'Then I'm glad too.'

In the evening the Talusi celebrated and feasted. Akenoro paused in his eating and said to Ba-umba.

'Such meat we have not eaten before.'

Ba-umba nodded and said :
'Matthew's sister brought it.'
'How can that be?' the young man demanded.
'I hunted and slew it by the river.'
'You must show me where. I'd hunt it too.'
'First you must learn.'
He laughed.

For two days Akenoro and his brothers sat in council with their father and the older men. Each time the meetings ended the men looked more serious.

'What's amiss, Matthew?'

'An old trouble in a new guise. Akenoro is cautious, unlike his brothers. He would wait – years if need be – to win all people to join the Talusi and move together. His brothers would move first and draw all others after.'

'Akenoro would ask leave of the Indians that lie in their path to cross their land. That means more delay. His brothers want to march and trust in their strength.'

'And what says Ba-umba?'

'He's at one with Akenoro – as are the older men.'

'And the young?'

'What thinkest thou?'

'I think all will go well, till Ba-umba dies.'

Matthew nodded.

When next Bess prepared to ride out to the cattle range, she saw Akenoro standing near.

'Good morrow, Bess.'

'Good morrow. What's your pleasure?'

'A man may greet his aunt, may he not?'

'Art impudent? Wouldst thou find favour with thine aunt?'

'I would.'

'Then call her not aunt.'

'Forgive me.'

'Gladly.'

'Wilt thou go hunt today?'

'Aye.'

'May I go with you?'

' 'Tis far and we shall ride.'

'I'll run beside thee.'

'Nay, Akenoro, that may not be. Do not offend the people.'

'I'll be judge of that.'

But in the end, the hunting party set out, with Akenoro mounted awkwardly on one of the horses. They rode slowly but he fell twice. Each time, gritting his teeth he mounted again. The young men grinned and muttered to each other. Akenoro replied amid more laughter.

'What do they say?'

'They say I am outfaced by a woman.'

'And what did thou reply?'

'Nay, 'twas by a horse.'

'Then thou must be master.'

'Of the woman?'

'No, the horse.'

Summer passed quickly. Bess, by her own reckoning, was now nineteen.

'Thy restlessness is strangely gone, Plymouth's forgotten,' said Matthew.

'Plymouth can bear my absence a while longer.'

'What of thy fortune?' he asked with slight malice.

'My guardians Trant and Rishworth, as our father once did say, will see to it as if it were their own.'

'And what will they say when thou return?'

'Trant at least will be ill-pleased. I'll wager he believes me dead and gone and is content with that. Heaven will have charge of my soul, he'll have charge of my fortune.'

'And you may not gainsay him?'

'He's my master till I'm five and twenty or I'm wed.'

'There must be many in Plymouth hot to wed Bess Morten and her fishing fleet.'

'Too many, but she's not on fire to wed. Nay, I'll go hunt and let who will go fish.'

'Take care thy quarry be not too great for thee.'

She laughed and left him. Later in the day she thought again about his words and was troubled a little. But riding through the forest, she forgot them.

Throughout the summer, Akenoro rode with Bess and the hunters. And often they would ride alone, leaving the others, roving deep into the forest, returning to the town in high spirits, to the curious glances of the women there. Or they would take a canoe and paddle across the bay, spear fish or swim from the headland.

'Art happy, Bess?' asked Matthew.

She nodded. He looked anxious.

'Be not too happy.'

'Why should I not?'

'For things that may not be.'

'Fret not. I make my ease.'

One day Bess persuaded Akenoro to sail out to Maravila Island. He needed little urging. They left the beach at dawn and with a fair wind and their paddles, reached the island by nightfall. Next day they roamed around the shore. Bess reckoned the island to be four miles square, with a fertile soil, forests, streams, inlets and a big, deep bay enclosed by rocky headlands.

Akenoro pointed to the bay.

'A fort there on the headland might hold off an Armada.'

They spent the day fishing and swimming in the clear water. As she bent over a rock pool Bess saw that her skin had now burned dark brown in the sun.

'I might pass for one of thy sisters.'

'Nay, not sister, nor aunt for that matter.'

'Am I not fair enough?'

'Too fair.'

She laughed and dived into the water. He followed, they fought and splashed. As it grew dark they built a fire, baked fish and watched the moon rise over the trees.

'Bess, when wilt thou return to thine own people?'

'I know not. Some day I will go.'

'Not soon.'

She gazed out to the sea.

'If I might have my way, I'd return to England and come back again with good people to make a home here. My people and thine would be friends...'

'I know... Matthew told me.'

She looked at his half-turned head.

'Does it displease thee?'

He shook his head. 'But 'tis not easy. I would not have thee go. Others would not have thee return.'

'I care not for others.'

'I do believe thee.' His mood changed. He took her hands. 'Shall we stay here?'

'Nay, we cannot sail at night.'

'Always a mocking answer.'

She bit her lip. 'Sometimes I fear to speak in earnest.'

He drew close to her. In a flash as his lips touched hers she thought she saw the dark face of Manuel and trembled. Then it vanished and her fears with it.

They returned to the mainland next day and for two weeks Bess did not see Akenoro. She hunted, but he did not ride with her. She did not see him again until Matthew and she ate supper with Ba-umba. Akenoro sat quietly nearby, smiled at her, but said little.

Ba-umba spoke to Bess. 'You like Maravila Island?'

'I do. 'Tis a fine spot. Men and women might live well there.'

He nodded.

'There are poor folks in England who might farm that land, raise crops, bring goods – trade with thy people,' she went on.

'What of the Spaniards?'

'The Spaniards' might is passing. They have no dominion over thy people. Together we need have no fear.'

B.   I

'Will thy people rest content to trade with mine or will they want more?'

'What does that mean?'

'It means I trust none of any people who make slaves of mine.'

'But these are poor. They enslave no one.'

He laughed harshly. 'A poor man who enslaves others may grow rich.'

' 'Twill not be so.'

'Thou sayest.'

Bess was about to reply angrily, but Matthew signalled silence. When he met her next day, his face was serious.

'Bess. Things go badly. I fear thou hast offended Ba-umba.'

'How can that be? Can he not bear his word to be disputed?'

'Ha, 'tis not his word, nor thine that is in question. 'Tis his son.'

'What is with Akenoro?'

'Thou art, too much.'

'That is not thy concern,' she said angrily.

'Oh, Bess, be warned. There is a mood among this people – of discontent. There's talk of thee already.'

'What harm have I done the people?'

'Nought but good. Let it remain so.'

Her anger gave way to heaviness of heart and it seemed Akenoro was avoiding her She sought him round the town but could not find him. Hurt, anger, a feeling of slight and insult blended inside her.

She did not see him again until an evening came when the young men and women danced together before the great lodge where Ba-umba sat with the elders of the Talusi. By him sat his sons, Akenoro among them. Bess, from her place beside Matthew, looked at the young man, but his eyes looked down and would not meet hers.

The drums beat louder and the dancers formed a double line

in the firelight, advancing and retreating. Bess stirred restlessly. Matthew laid his hand on hers.

'He shall see me,' she said passionately.

She threw off Matthew's hand and sprang into the centre, joining the young women as they swayed to and fro. Still Akenoro did not raise his head. Keeping time with the dance she moved across to him and stretched out to seize his hands.

Ba-umba stood, raised his hand. The drumming stopped and the dancers fell back. His face was hard; his voice was calm.

'It may not be,' he said.

'Why?' asked Bess defiantly.

'You are not of our people.'

'Matthew is not of your people.'

'For us Matthew can do no wrong. Akenoro must lead his people. It may not be.'

Ba-umba turned to Matthew. 'It is enough. She must go.'

Akenoro sprang to his feet, grief and anger in his face. Matthew rose and faced Ba-umba.

'I shall go, too.'

From the people nearby came an anxious muttering. Ba-umba controlled his rage.

'We will talk tomorrow,' he said and strode away into his house.

Bess woke from a broken, dream-ridden sleep next morning to find two men at her door. They led her across the town square to Ba-umba's house. The chief sat in his own doorway, with Matthew and two of the older men beside him. Akenoro and his brothers were nowhere to be seen.

Ba-umba nodded to her and she sat down. He began to speak slowly in his own language. Matthew translated.

'Ba-umba is angry but will not drive thee away. Thou art the Talusi's friend and helper. But thy ways are strange and the people are perplexed.'

'I did not intend harm,' said Bess quietly.

'He bids thee stay. Or go in peace if so minded. He has spoken with the elders. They say that if thy folk will settle on Maravila, they will not hinder it. It may be that they will be your allies.'

'I am grateful,' she replied.

'He bids thee, still in friendship, not to seek after Akenoro.'

'But how if Akenoro seek after me?'

Ba-umba heard this calmly. He said in English, 'Akenoro is not his own man. He belongs to his people.'

'I would not own him. But cherish him.'

'Art thou in child with him?'

'Nay!' the answer burst out.

He nodded, spoke again in Talusi.

'He bids thee take to thyself a young man. There are many among the hunters who would gladly . . .'

'Suitors I may have in Plymouth. I want but one . . .'

'Nay, Bess, thou may not.' Matthew spoke on his own.

'Oh, I may not. To thee, my brother, the chief's sister to wed. But to me, thy sister, not the chief's son.'

She stood up. 'Good brother. Good lord Ba-umba. 'Tis clear I can't command. 'Tis clear I'll not submit. So I must depart. I'll not outstay my welcome. I'll wait but for the next Dutch vessel that sails by.'

Ba-umba nodded. 'I thank thee.'

'May I not see Akenoro once more?'

'Akenoro is gone away. He will return in time . . .'

'When I am gone?'

Ba-umba said nothing. Bess turned slowly and walked away. Matthew followed her to the thorn bush corral where horses were kept. He looked at her tense face and tight-set lips.

'Bess, break not thy heart. There's life to live in plenty.'

She combed her horse's mane with her fingers.

'Fear not, brother. I'll not rage as men are wont to do nor weep as women are bidden. I'll find another way.'

She swung on to the horse's back and rode into the forest.

Chapter eighteen

The Dutch ship, her holds crammed with salt for the herring fleets of Middleburg, and dyewood for France, sailed from Maravila where she had taken on fresh water. The captain had asked no questions when the Cimaroons had brought a passenger. They paid well in stolen Spanish gold. And if he failed them, he knew not to return that way, for they had long memories.

His passenger gave no trouble; a good sailor who complained neither of the rolling of the ship nor the food. She kept to herself and said little, though he knew she spoke a little Dutch. He saw she was looked after and left her alone, though sometimes he eyed her as she walked the deck and wondered. There was a sad air about her, masked by pride.

Bess was content to be alone with her memories and her thoughts. At night there were memories of Matthew bidding her farewell – 'Please God we'll meet again, if only in Utopia'; of Ba-umba, grave and silent, standing on the shore; of the hunters crowding round with gifts, a tasselled lance, a plaited bridle, a decorated shell horn. And of Akenoro – his stricken face in the firelight.

During the day there were thoughts and plans. With Matthew's aid she had mapped Maravila island. There were, she guessed, some three thousand acres of fertile land for cultivation, maybe as many again for pasture. Tobacco would grow there well, so would cassava, plantain and the pine-fruit, oranges, bananas. Merchants' and gentlemen's wives in England would pay well for the fruits, and their husbands for the tobacco. A hundred might farm there and live well. With Cimaroon help, or even without it, cattle could be brought from the mainland.

They'd need a vessel, 300 tons or more, something bigger than Morten fishing vessels to carry the colonists and their stores and tools. Timber there was in plenty on the island.

She'd have Tom Curnock as her skipper. And Martin Fletcher might sail with them, to teach and pray. With Sam Fletcher's help, she'd find a lawyer who would see to getting charters and patents to settle. It might take a year, or two or more, yet let it once be started and it would succeed.

One thing was uncertain. What would her guardians think of her plan? Rishworth she knew she could persuade. But Trant must be made to see the Lord's will in the project, plus some return for the estate. And return there could be, with two harvests a year. In four or five years all money laid out might be returned with interest.

If she had to wait until she had command over her estate before she began, then that would mean ten years. And in ten years, what might have happened? The Talusi, and Matthew, might be utterly gone from the Darien shore. And that she did not dare think about.

'I must win over Mr Trant,' she told herself. 'Be patient and biddable, Bess Morten. No high words, no tantrums. Learn to sing small as poor Ben Moore needed now and then. Be a model of virtue and modesty.'

She laughed aloud at her own thoughts and the captain, sitting in his cabin next door, wondered again about his passenger.

It was a good time of year. The ship caught the westerlies above the Bahamas, and forged steadily through the Atlantic rollers. Bess walked on deck in the sunshine, marked the steady speed of the ship, heard the captain promise they'd be in the Channel in fifteen days, and felt her excitement grow.

As they drew into the Channel, the skipper, himself eager to be home, gained Bess's agreement to a change of plans.

'In these winds, your good port of Plymouth is like Satan's stronghold, easy to enter, but hard to leave.'

He signalled a passing wine ship bound for Exeter and saw Bess safely aboard before setting course again for Middleburg. He took from her letters to Matthew and Akenoro, which he promised would be delivered next spring when he sailed back to Maravila. And he handed to her a portion of the money he received, to see her home.

The wine carriers viewed the dark woman, in her elegant though creased Spanish dress and cape, with some curiosity, and her strange, scanty baggage with suspicion. But when they knew she was from Plymouth they were more friendly. The captain had known her father slightly. He wagged his head.

'The fishing trade is fallen off these past two years. Barbary raiders steal the fishermen and London merchants steal the profit. But there's wealth in Plymouth still, lady. They've built a new Guildhall, roofed in the Market Place, plenty of gold ribbon in ladies' hats, blackamoor servants to walk behind. Piped water's all the fashion for those that can pay. Though,' he chuckled, 'last winter all the pipes did burst in the frost.'

'Know you of Mr Trant and Mr Rishworth, my guardians?'

'The names I know, lady, but nought else. Still, we'll be in port tomorrow, and on Friday ye may ride with the carrier. A rolling ride, seven hours of it, but you're a good sailor.'

But once in Exeter Bess found a coastal bark was bound for Plymouth. She took no rest but boarded it and sailed within the hour. The winds were contrary and the skipper, it seemed, not fully sober, but, as the next day dawned, Bess found herself sailing into Sutton Pool, home again after nearly five years.

Five years had changed the port. New warehouses and cranes crowded the quays and beyond them, new bastions were added to the walls. On shore the old familiar bustle round the jetties was beginning and there at the New Quay, two of her father's old fishing boats – her fishing boats – were tied up.

As the vessel bumped against the harbour wall, she turned impatiently to the sailor who stood ready to carry her baggage ashore, and, snatching the bundles, leapt from thwart to steps in a quick bound. A dozen hasty strides took her to the quay amid the stares of labourers and sailors. She took no notice, but pushed on through the crowd. There was the end of Vauxhall Street now. A turn to the left and she would be in Stillman Street and see her home again

The crowd had grown thicker near the end of the wharf. Voices called her, plaintively.

'Alms, sweet lady, for Jesu's sake.'

'I've no coin,' she answered. Head bent she forced her way forward. But the voices followed, hands were thrust before her. Two women stood in her path, babies at the breast.

'Alms, lady, not for me, for the child.'

'Truly, I've no money. My voyage cost me all I had,' answered Bess. 'But come to my door in Stillman Street, within the hour.'

'Stillman Street?'

'Aye, the Morten house.'

The women were suddenly silent, then one called, 'Charity left that house long ago.'

Bess stopped. That voice plucked at her memory as the hands plucked at her sleeve. She looked into the face, the dark hair held under a faded kerchief.

The woman stared back in bewilderment. 'I know your voice, lady, but the face is changed.'

'And I know yours. What is thy name?'

'What's it to you? We've done no wrong. We all have licence to beg in the port.'

'I mean you no harm, truly. But tell me your name.'

'Judith Curnock, an it please you.'

Bess's heart stopped. She dropped one bundle, reached out to touch the weathered face.

The woman flinched. 'Nay, leave my child.'

'I would not harm thee, sweet Judith, nor thy child, for all the world. Dost thou not know me?'

'I know not . . .'

'Judith, I am Bess Morten.'

Judith spoke rapidly: 'That cannot be. She's gone beyond the seas. She's dead for sure. Young Martin Fletcher followed in her path, when she did vanish. She was taken none knows where . . .'

' 'Tis true? Martin did seek me?'

Judith gazed at her. Her voice trembled. 'Art thou truly Bess Morten?'

'As thou art Judith Curnock.'

'Thank God thou art alive.' She came close and touched the dark face with her free hand. 'How thou art changed.'

Bess put her arms around Judith. 'Things have gone ill for thee Judith. But where is Tom?'

'Taken last year by Sallee Rovers. Two ships sunk, two seized, some slain and others taken captive.'

'And these poor women?'

'Likewise, wives and children, of Morten crews. Thy crews, Bess.'

'Aye, lady,' called a woman behind her, 'thy crews.'

'But Judith. Why art thou not at Coppins' with thy child?'

Judith laughed harshly, 'Father and mother died. The lease ended. It went to a neighbour who bid more than Crispin could.'

'Where's Crispin?'

'Married and gone to Virginia.'

'And thy sisters?'

'One married, gone to live away. One's in the service of the Daunceys. They gave her employment for thy sake.'

Bess looked round at the women and children. There were some twenty of them.

'You shall all with me to Stillman Street, and have to eat.'

'We've been turned from that door too often.'

'How can that be?'

'While Trant and his beldame rule the roost, that's why.'

'But what of Rishworth?'

'Poor soul, he's dead. His heart did fail him.'

'Aye, it always did.'

'What of his wife?'

'She lives with her sister down in Plympton.'

'Enough,' said Bess and snatched up her bundle. 'We will to Stillman Street.' She set off along Vauxhall Street, Judith at her side and the others following. They turned into Stillman Street.

The old house was the same. No, the Broad Chamber windows were new-leaded and the wall above freshly plastered. Judith saw Bess's glance.

'Aye, Mr Trant has seen well to it. Men and women go down in price, bricks and mortar advance.'

Bess led them through the gate into the courtyard, and pushed open the kitchen door. Inside the fire burned in the range. A woman in a white apron was pinning chickens on a long spit before it, while another stirred a pot hung over the blaze. A third stood by the old scrubbed table, cutting vegetables. All three turned round. Bess knew none of them. The woman at the pot stood up.

'What will you, lady?'

'Is that stew ready? It smells good.'

'It is. Mr Trant will eat at noon with gentlemen from the town.'

'Their need's not great. See, what's thy name?'

'Eleanor, madam.'

'Then, good Eleanor, bear that broth into the courtyard and do you others bring plates and serve my guests.'

'But lady. How may I do that? Mr Trant will not

allow . . .' She peered through the kitchen doorway. 'I know these women. They've had charity at his hands before now.'

'Aye, and will have more at mine.'

'But, who . . . ?'

'My name is Morten and this house is mine.'

'Your name I know, lady, but Mistress Morten's no more. 'Tis Mistress Trant that orders the household now.'

'We'll see. Now, wilt thou serve the broth or shall I?'

'I know not how I may. Mr Trant will be wroth.'

Bess strode to the fireplace, took up a cloth and lifting two-handed, swung the pot from its hook. Then as the cook and her maids gazed open-mouthed, she carried it into the courtyard. In a few minutes all the women and children were eating. As they ate, their chatter grew louder till the courtyard filled with noise.

'What is this babble? Who bid these people enter?'

On the gallery landing above stood Mistress Trant, her gaunt face furious, her white hair seeming to bristle. Bess rose, one of the children in her arms, and went to the foot of the stairs.

'Good morrow, Mistress Trant. We have company to breakfast.'

'Is this some jest, madam? I know these women. They have received my charity, but they are not allowed within these gates.'

'What is more,' she went on, 'before I have my servants see them out, I would know by what right you brought them in.'

Bess looked up at Alice Trant. 'What right? My name is Morten and this is my house.'

The woman opened her mouth, shrieked 'Mordecai!' and fainted.

Chapter nineteen

Moments later Bess confronted Mordecai Trant in the Broad Chamber, her feelings bursting out in a storm of rage. But Trant met her storming with a rock-like calm giving one answer to all her accusations and protests.

'Thy father's will gave Mr Rishworth and myself full charge of his affairs, to manage till thou should reach five and twenty, or until thou marry. Now Mr Rishworth is no more, I bear the trust alone. Bear it I will.'

'Whether I like it or not?'

'These past five years thy likes and dislikes have been unknown to me. But I did pledge thy father I'd protect thy fortune. And this despite the turns and twists of trade I've done. Let us but go into the counting house and I will make account to thee. Thy fortune is not less, but more.'

'Nay, Mr Trant, I'd not accuse thee of false accounting. But did my father bid thee thwart me?'

'He did bid me serve thine interests for he feared that oft thou knowest them not thyself. But, say, what has been done ill?'

'Why hast thou not helped Judith Curnock and the other wives and families?'

'They have had relief till thy estate will not bear more. Two ships lie in port for lack of crew and earn nothing. Others are lost.'

'That is not their blame.'

'Nor mine. The rovers from the Barbary coast have taken

their husbands. We have entreated many times – Vice-Admiral, the Court, the King himself. We've sent petitions from the town. Nothing is done. Devon men are in corsair hands and the navy rots in port.'

'Has no one tried to ransom our men?'

'Aye. The price is high – sixty pound a head and more. Each time we inquire, the price is higher. Our men alone would cost a thousand pounds to ransom.'

'Then we must pay the cost.'

'But thy estate in fee for it, I'll not do it.'

'The trust you hold for me is hard – on them.'

' 'Tis hard, I know. But thy estate must be protected.'

'Despite what others lose?'

'Aye,' said Trant grimly. 'In thy absence, I had to go to court on thy behalf. Lady Ferrers, thy father's cousin, would have thee presumed dead and claim thy fortune as thy kin.'

Bess rose from the table and walked to the window. If Lady Ferrers could not have her for Ralph, she'd have the estate. She shivered and turned to Trant.

'And thou didst affirm I was alive?'

'I did.'

'And knew not?'

'We sent young Fletcher to inquire after thee.'

Bess looked out at the harbour. Martin had followed her.

'Where is Master Fletcher now, and his father?'

'No longer with us. Sam Fletcher lives in Tavistock. He has a pension from the estate.'

'And Martin?'

'He went his way. He thought he'd found signs of thee in Bristol. He would have me charter a ship that he might follow after.'

'But thou didst not agree.'

'Send a ship to America, after a roving boy called Ben Moore, in the hopes he'd turn out to be a young lady called Bess Morten?'

'Not worth the pain,' said Bess ironically.

Trant rose and faced her from the middle of the room.

'I did not await thy thanks for ought that I have done. But the estate's secure. In five years' time, or when thou'rt wed, it's thine to use or cast away. But . . .' he paused and said slowly. 'Think not thou canst command without the means to do it.'

'I see 'tis fruitless to dispute, Mr Trant. But tell me was it for my protection that you live in my house?'

For a second Trant looked uncomfortable. He turned to the table and stroked the heavy cloth.

'We deemed it best to keep this house up and put our own to rent.'

'Tell me, Mr Trant, how may I win a husband, if I cannot manage my own household?'

He looked away. 'We'll turn to our own house as soon as we may end the lease.'

'And for the upkeep of this one?'

'There is allowance from the estate.'

'And I may choose my own servants?'

'Thou shalt be mistress in thine own house.'

'Margaret Bray. Where is she?' asked Bess suddenly.

'She's gone away. I know not where. She and Ned Wallis . . .'

'Ned?'

'Aye. Their manner was shameless. Mistress Trant would not have them under her roof.'

Bess laughed. 'Well done Margaret. Well done Ned. Who would have thought?'

He stiffened. 'No man is too old for mischief, nor woman neither. Now, with thy leave, I'll to my work. Perchance tomorrow, we'll go more into these matters.'

With that he left her.

Bess sent word to Judith to bring old Will Curnock to lodge in Stillman Street. But Judith was unwilling to leave the other wives, who lived in lodgings near the Dung Quay.

'Never fear,' Bess told her, 'I'll find the means to help them – aye, and rescue the menfolk.'

'Brave words, Bess.'

'I was ever bold, Judith.'

' 'Tis gold we need, not boldness.'

'That we shall have,' said Bess firmly. She spoke confidently for Judith's sake. Much had changed in five years, she thought. Then she had been fearless – for her own sake, but now she must be steadfast – for the sake of others.

Bess sat down and wrote letters to Samuel Fletcher and Margaret Bray, asking them to return to her service. In ten days she had answers. From Margaret came a dignified note, signed 'Mrs Wallis'. It expressed joy at her safe return but added, 'We make a small living, Mr Wallis by copying, I by teaching letters to husbandmen's children. Please God we may flourish – in a small way. But we are content.'

Sam Fletcher sent warm greetings – 'Thank God who preserved thee, Mistress Elizabeth,' but excused himself on account of his age. He added 'Thy return will gladden the heart of my son.'

'Nothing for it, Bess. Shift for thyself,' she said.

She bought new clothes and set out to call on all the leading merchants and captains of the town and their wives, begging them to subscribe money to a ransom fund. Trant, embarrassed, if not ashamed, headed the list with £100. Others gave smaller sums, some willingly, some grudgingly. Yet others were caustic. 'Are we to ransom your servants, Mistress Morten? Let Trant open the purse strings a little wider.'

Others were sceptical. 'Ransom's been tried before. Cast not good money after bad. Put it rather in the fund for orphans.'

'Ye count their fathers lost, then?'

'Until the King's ships be sent to burn the Sallee Rovers as their galleys burned our ships, there'll be no end on't. If we pay ransom, the corsairs will raise their price. Cast not good money after bad.'

The bland, serious faces of the merchants, sympathetic or hostile, angered Bess. But not so much as the pursed lips of their wives. She knew that as soon as she left them, they turned to their gossip – 'Tired of roving the country playing the man, she comes back to pick our pockets. She needs a firm hand – she needs a husband's hand, neighbour. Aye, but who will have her – a beanpole with a blackamoor's face? Plenty, I'm told. Nay, 'tis her fortune, not her face, they seek.'

After two months' visiting, arguing and pleading, Bess had collected £240. Enough, if the price had not risen in Algiers, to ransom four men. Judith said bitterly: 'But which four?'

By August Bess had pleaded with every family of means in the port and some outside and had begun to feel her confidence and patience were at an end. Then quite suddenly came a relief.

She sat one morning in the Broad Chamber, her lists before her, when a servant knocked on the door.

'A man to see you, Mistress.'

'What manner of man?'

'I know not, a mechanic perchance.'

Bess went into the gallery. A man in his twenties, thin and hollow-cheeked, but tidily dressed, hose darned and pockets patched, woollen cap in his hand, stood in the courtyard. He looked up. Their eyes met, stared a moment, then:

'Martin.'

'Bess.'

He hesitated, then came swiftly up the stairs. He took her outstretched hand and bowed over it. He followed her into the Broad Chamber.

'Sit down, Martin. Where hast thou been in the world?'

'Well I might ask thee that.'

'I command thee. Speak first.'

'I've been about, in the Eastern Counties and the Low Countries. Some of our church fled across the sea, their wives and children were seized. We sought to help them. Now all's well, for all are together, in Leyden City.'

'Will they not return?' asked Bess.

'Nay. All must now conform and go by the bishop's rules. More praying, less preaching is how it goes. And woe betide those who interpret the Word in their own way.'

'Why should they be so hot against it?'

'If people worship in their own way, Bess, then Jack may be his own Minister. If Jack's his own priest, who needs a bishop? If bishops go out of fashion, what of Lords and Kings?'

'But, Martin, that is perilous work for thee.'

'They can but crop my ears. And I'm told 'twould make me less ill-favoured.'

'Martin, who dares say thou art ill-favoured?'

He blushed.

'But, now thou'rt come...'

'Father wrote me. Thou'rt in need of help.'

She laid her hand on his.

'Bless thee, Martin Fletcher. But thy payment will be small. I'm not mistress of my fortune for five years.'

He smiled, 'My keep will do, and one thing more.'

'What's that?'

'Ben Moore will tell me all?'

It was her turn to blush.

'Ben Moore will tell thee much, perhaps Bess Morten less.'

'Well, what is your need, Mistress Morten?'

Bess told him briefly. He nodded as she spoke.

'Thou hast done well, to charm so much gold from such tight pockets. But, 'tis a waste of time, I fear.'

'I fear so.'

'Bess, we can try among the sailors and fisherfolk themselves, the apprentices and so forth. We'll speak in church about it.'

'They have but little wealth.'

'But there are many.'

'We can but try.'

'Now secondly. These wives who lack their men. Charity will help them starve slowly. In the end such doles sour taker as well as giver. What they must have is work.'

'What work may they do?'

'Can they not spin? I'll go see the woolmen into the next hundred if need be. Father and I know men there who'll do a good turn, if it turn to their good in the end. Haply Father and I can teach the stronger ones to weave. I can find old looms. We'll need a cottage with a large room.' He sprang up and walked about.

'But the Mayor, the Corporation will say "Nay!"'

'Then we'll go outside the city. 'Tis done everywhere now. A plague on their regulations if folk shall starve.'

'Ben Moore says Amen to that.'

By the autumn, Martin had done his work, walking, riding here and there, writing letters. Before winter set in, all the fisherwives were working, earning enough to keep themselves and their children. At first Bess often went to the cottage to see them and marvelled at their cheerfulness. Soon she realized that though they were grateful, they had little need of her company. She felt apart and almost envied them the warmth and friendship of their little group.

'Why, 'tis a miracle, Martin,' she said.

'Aye, please God the wool market holds,' he said soberly.

But the ransom money grew slowly. By spring, despite their efforts, there was no more than £300.

Bess said to Martin: 'When I came home I had but a single dream and plan. Now I have nought but burdens which I shift on to you.'

'Talk not of burdens, Bess. Tell me rather of thy dream.'

Bess told Martin of Maravila, though some impulse made her say nothing of Akenoro. She told him of her talks with Matthew, of her vision of a little place 'where men might make their ease.'

' 'Tis a fine thing, Bess. It has thy stamp upon it. 'Twould cost a fortune to begin it though, in the manner you propose.'

'And on that I'd bestow my fortune – if I had it to command. I would do much to have it in my power.'

'What? Would'st marry a plump lawyer's son? Then thy burden's soon lifted.'

'Art saucy, Martin. I might indeed – if I could be sure he'd leave me to dispose my fortune where I would.'

'And what man acceptable to Mr Trant would do that?'

' 'Tis true, Martin,' she sighed, ' – if I were a man.'

'Nay, Bess, mar not nature's work.'

'Now thou art truly saucy.'

Chapter twenty

One spring day, Bess rode out to visit the Daunceys. She found them well enough, though hard-pressed for money. Hugh was inclined to take their troubles calmly. Not so Mary. She gave voice to her indignation to Bess.

'Ploughmen may get drunk, sleep late and stay from church. None think of them. Puritans may wander hither and thither seeking new wonders from this lecturer and that. But when our family stays from church for conscience's sake, we are pursued with fines.'

'Nay, Mary,' said Hugh, ' 'tis no easier for the other sort, God knows. King and Bishops will have no straying from the path – either towards Rome or Geneva. But we are known, this family has a name, and for it we must pay.'

'How has it been, Hugh?' asked Bess.

' 'Twas bad four years ago after the plot against Parliament. Some of our faith were driven out, some priests were hanged. Some fled to Spain and conspire there, but I will none of that. My country and my faith, why should they be divided?'

'Amen to that,' said Bess.

'We've heard talk of thy fantastic journeyings up and down the earth. But what since thy return?'

Bess told them of her work to raise the ransom for the Barbary corsair's prisoners.

They listened with sympathy, then, suddenly Mary said, as though reminded: 'Hast seen ought of Sir Ralph since thy return?'

'*Sir* Ralph?'

'Aye. Sir Charles is dead, rest his soul. Ralph carries the title!'

'That he does,' said Hugh, 'far and wide!'

'What may that mean?'

Mary laughed. 'Hugh takes it ill, that his cousin will not stay and walk about his land, but plays the privateer.'

'I take it ill that the estate, poor as it is, should be in debt to fit out ships for ventures that bring nought.'

'That is not so,' said Mary warmly. 'Ralph has had prizes worth the name. Why, one was sold for two thousand but twelve months since.'

'Aye, and where has it gone?'

'Best not to ask,' said Mary and Bess nodded.

'I've seen Sir Ralph at pleasure with his man in Sutton harbour,' she said.

'Francis Durmer?' said Hugh, 'now there's a strange creature. He's followed Ralph through thick and thin these past seven years.'

'Follow?' said Mary. 'Nay, Durmer's ever ready to point the path. Ralph has the will and Durmer shows the way.'

These words stayed in Bess's mind. No more than three weeks later, sitting at her window, she saw a flash of green in the road beneath, from the cloak of a horseman. As he stopped before the house, and dismounted, Bess recognized the young-old face, the bald head, the curving eyebrows. A moment later, a servant told her Mr Durmer asked to be allowed to see her.

Durmer entered the chamber, flat velvet hat held before him, and bowed low, waiting near the door.

'Mistress Morten.'

'What is your errand?' Bess was cool.

' 'Tis something of the utmost privacy.'

'Then close the door and come forward, if you please.'

He closed the door but remained deferentially standing a little way from the table.

'I'm come for my master, Sir Ralph Ferrers. He wishes to offer help.'

Bess kept her astonishment hidden. She felt Durmer watched her face keenly, though his eyes were lowered.

'Help. In what?'

'I will be brief. The matter of the Sallee Rovers's captives. My master has a plan to free the men, or some of them.'

'How, can he raise the ransom? One thousand pounds for our fishermen alone.'

The shadow of a smile moved on Durmer's face.

'No, my lady. His is not the diplomatic way.'

'That I did not suppose. But speak up, Mr Durmer. If there's a way, I'd try it.'

He nodded, 'The Sallee Rovers, now the weather's fair, will venture up into the Channel. These days they come on shore and put the torch to villages – as they did in Cornwall last year.'

'But how . . . ?'

'Indeed, madam. They are so bold because they fear no counter-blow. And they bring captives with them, some willingly as renegadoes, some by force, to guide them in.'

'I do begin to see,' said Bess.

'My master said you would.'

'How will your master help?'

'He has a ship, the *Charles*, named for our young prince of whom there are high hopes one day.'

Durmer's voice grew a fraction warmer. 'It is a flyer, and besides, 'tis well armed with a crew that's handy . . .' he paused as though coming to a delicate point.

'Would your master hire himself as ransom earner?'

Durmer nodded: 'After a fashion. He proposes to lie out along the coast. We are not ill-informed in these matters . . .'

'In corsair matters, no, I trow . . .'

'And will engage to board the Rovers one by one, set free the captives . . .'

'But we can no more pay him ransom than we can the Turk. We have but £300.'

Durmer raised his hand. 'My master knows this. The truth is he'll engage himself if only for enough money to get the *Charles* to sea. Once there his sport's reward enough for him.'

'Say, Mr Durmer. What do you think of this business?'

He raised his eyes – light grey ones – and looked shrewdly at Bess.

'I think there is no profit in it. But I am my master's man and he will do it . . .'

'Why, Mr Durmer, why?'

He hesitated, then said: 'For five years since the truce with Spain, Sir Ralph has got his letters of marque against our foes, from the Prince of Orange. Before long, even this year perhaps, there will be truce in the Low Countries. Where shall he go then for licence to privateer? To the Duke of Savoy, perhaps. But these matters take time. He will have action now.'

'Frankly spoken, Mr. Durmer. I understand. Tell your master, I will think upon this proposition for which I thank him . . .' she saw his face '. . . there's more?'

'There is, lady. He has a second plan. That he should take hostages from each Rover galley – men of price, no other. The hostages he'll lodge with each town which hath men captive. And he is sure that 'ere long, perhaps by the good offices of Spain and her ambassador, Algiers will make exchange.'

'There's risk there, but a chance,' said Bess.

When Durmer left, agreeing to return in two days' time, she sent a servant to bring Martin and told him what Ferrers's man had said. Martin shook his head wonderingly.

'A rare plan. If it would work. Canst thou trust these men?'

'Master and man. 'Tis a spin of the coin which I trust

less. But Martin,' her voice sharpened, 'I'd liefer take that chance than sit here, while our men sit there.'

If Martin had doubts Judith and the other wives had none. Said Judith: 'If I were a man, I'd sail aboard that craft and board with the rest.'

Made cautious by experience, Bess spoke also to Trant. He made clear his disapproval, but said: 'I know that if I forbid it, thou will only employ Fletcher to act on thy behalf and set the scheme afoot. But, if the money's lost, as lost it well may be, I will not engage to find more.'

Bess was content with that and next day, when Durmer came, she told him briefly that she would use the ransom money to fit the *Charles* for sea.

'But one condition, Mr Durmer.'

'Madam?'

'Mr Fletcher and I will sail with her. I'll not go blindfold into this.'

'My lady, we have never sailed with women on board.'

'Say to Sir Ralph; I'll dress in men's clothes, come armed, and be discreet. I'll not hinder his crew at their labours.'

He bowed. A week later came word that the *Charles* was ready at an inlet down the coast. Ferrers would not come into Plymouth harbour, finding his debts with the port authorities an embarrassment. Another week passed then came another message. It was brief: 'Sallee Rovers off the Lizard. We sail on the dawn tide.'

Bess and Martin arrived at the cove at daybreak next day to find the *Charles* at anchor. Bess nodded her approval at the rakish cut of the ship, and when they boarded her from a small boat, half an hour later, she noted the burnished cannon all well trimmed. No wonder the Ferrers estate was in pawn. All they had was invested in this ship.

Ferrers waited as they came aboard, Durmer close behind him. He bowed low but kept his distance.

'We've news that half a dozen sails are sighted heading for

Fowey, Mistress Morten,' he said, 'my crew and I await your word.'

'Then my word is make all speed, Sir Ralph,' she said.

The crew, at their stations, heard her words and sent up a cheer. Ferrers turned to give orders, while Durmer conducted Bess and Martin to the poop. She felt the crew eye her as she swung nimbly up the deck ladders.

The boatswain doffed his cap: 'We're set for Dodmean's Point, my lady. With luck we'll get betwixt them and the wind by five o'clock and come upon them out of the sun.'

The bosun was right. Towards the end of the afternoon when the sun, large and red, was reaching down the western sky, he came again, doffed his cap and said: 'Sir Ralph's compliments. Here's a spy-glass he got secretly out of Amsterdam. You may see them from afar off, even before they see us.'

Wondering, Bess took the glass. In the circle of the lens, seeming almost in front of them, were six craft, moving slowly in line and heading for the coast to the north. As she handed back the glass, she heard Ferrers shout his orders, and the *Charles* glided through the water towards the unsuspecting Rovers.

The action lasted no more than an hour. The *Charles*, foam boiling beneath her bows, came on the first Rover out of the sun almost before its crew were aware of it. The galleys scattered in confusion, but none could match the speed and nimbleness of the *Charles*, which seemed to turn on its heel like a whippet after hares.

A single cannonade halted the nearest two, one with its main-mast splintered, one holed in the bows. The *Charles* closed in, raking the decks. Bess saw the crews diving overboard in panic.

Almost before the vessels' sides had touched, Ferrers was on to the prize at the head of a boarding party. Bess watched him leap across. Whatever his faults, Ferrers had no fears. Far from it; in every furious action, every vicious thrust of his sword blade as he fought his way into the Rover's demoralized crew, there was zest, a schoolboy's glee.

'We're boarded,' shouted the bosun. 'Pikes and pistols, lads.' Then all was confusion as the *Charles*, surrounded by the galleys like a bear by hounds, became itself the battle-ground. Three sailors ran up on to the poop, cutlasses raised and stationed themselves by the rail, waving Bess and Martin back. As they did, dark faces showed themselves not six feet away, and half-naked Rovers leapt to the deck. Then it was over and the deck was cleared. Two corsairs lay dead, Ferrers's men were helping a wounded mate from the poop.

Helped up by Martin, Bess looked around. Close to the *Charles*, three galleys were sinking, the sea alive with struggling men. The other Rovers were escaping with what speed they could. Ferrers's men were scouring the captured ships, seeking hostages and prisoners to release. There were shouts for a blacksmith to strike off chains from men at the oars below.

Before the sun had set, the *Charles* was under way again, leaving behind her only the corsair wreckage. Bess sat in the cabin with Ferrers and Martin. Durmer and the bosun stood near the door.

'What is our tally, Sir Ralph?' she asked.

'Well worth the venture,' Ferrers answered, watching her carefully. 'Forty men set free, though fifteen others died in the action. And we have taken a dozen hostages.'

'I would go see the men who are freed,' Bess said.

'Gladly. I'm told there are fifteen from Plymouth.'

More than that, there were six of her father's old crews, haggard men, in rags, their faces still showing their amazement at their escape from the galley. When they knew who she was, one knelt and kissed her hand.

She drew the man, old enough to be her father, up from the deck: 'Good friends, you will be home, 'ere dawn.'

The weeks that followed showed that Ferrers's gamble

had its shrewd side. More than one grateful town or shipmaster hastened to make gifts in repayment for the men who were freed. As the money flowed in, Durmer showed his first signs of excitement, but Ferrers, now that the fighting was over, seemed indifferent to the rewards. Bess sensed that the man now only looked forward to the next engagement.

There was not long to wait. The *Charles*, ranging the Channel north of Ushant, surprised three more corsairs, and brought home more hostages and more freed Devon men. Of the Morten men, only Judith's Tom and seven others remained captive. And Durmer reckoned that enough hostages were held to make it worth their while to sound out the possibilities of an exchange.

A time of waiting followed which bore hard on the strained patience of Judith and the other wives, an impatience that affected Bess and Martin too. But they could do no more, but only wait. The *Charles* sailed back to her inlet, and Ferrers and his men went back to their amusements.

After a month came word that an exchange would be made, twenty for twenty, Devon men for corsair captives. Durmer rode over to Stillman Street to report.

'A meeting's proposed, south of the Lizard – one vessel for either side. But not the *Charles*. They'll not have that. They want one of their own weight.'

'Then we'll send a fishing vessel.'

'Such did Sir Ralph have in mind . . .'

'What else . . .'

'This. Not to trust them. There'll be some ruse.'

'What's his intent, then?'

'To have the *Charles* in the offing, concealed beyond a point to guard against treachery.'

'What treachery?'

'That they may take on board their men and hold ours and thus escape.'

'Very well. But it's to be understood, the *Charles* will come in only if we signal.'

'It's understood. A single pistol shot.'

At dawn on the agreed day, Bess, Martin, and a well-armed crew of men from the port, aboard a Morten fishing vessel, waited in an inlet near the Lizard Point. The corsair vessel had been observed ten miles out, the night before, and the *Charles*, well hidden, waited beyond the headland.

At six, the corsair hove in sight and, slackening speed, drifted nearer. A white flag was hoisted and Bess signed for her crew to do the same. When both vessels were fifty yards apart, the captives were brought out on deck, linked together five at a time. Bess saw the men lined on the corsair deck and tried without success to pick out Tom Curnock. He must still be below.

The crew stood to arms as the vessels came together. There was a pause as men on each side picked out their own. Then at a signal, bonds were cut, and five captives from each side rushed forward and were helped into their own ship. Bess felt the breath leave her lungs in a rush, and commanded the next five to be brought on deck.

Again the exchange. But still no Tom. Tenseness returned to her body. Some faint far-away movement made her turn. Above the headland she could see the top-mast of the *Charles*. A flash of white – were they hoisting sail?

Now fifteen men had been exchanged. No sign of Tom. Bess had the last five corsair captives brought on deck. Then she saw Tom amid his mates – no mistake there.

Suddenly the corsair captain shouted.

Before the Devon men could move, the corsair captives leapt into their own ship, where Tom and his mates were being hustled below. On the corsair ship the crew ran hither and thither, throwing off the grappling irons that held the two ships together, raising sail. Some shouted and pointed.

'Look – the *Charles*,' shouted Martin.

Ferrers's ship, full sail, was rounding the point, as the corsair ship drew off.

'Tom. They've taken Tom,' cried Bess.

In that instant the *Charles* opened fire. The corsair, caught full amidships, opened up and began to sink.

'In God's name,' screamed Bess, 'rescue them.'

Her ship was on the move, already bearing down on the sinking corsair, whose decks were awash. Heads bobbed in the water. The corsair vessel split and vanished as the water boiled like a cooking pot. Crew men leaned over the side, grappling for drowning bodies, plucking at shirts, hair, anything their fingers could grasp. Then it was over, the sea littered with planks and rope.

Two Devon men had drowned, but by a miracle, Tom and two others had been saved.

Chapter twenty-one

Tom and his shipmates were with their families again by nightfall, and there were celebrations in every inn around the harbour. The *Charles*, her debts to the port forgotten, was moored in Sutton Pool and her crew were toasted and cheered until the dawn began to show, though her captain was nowhere to be seen. With Francis Durmer, Ferrers had quietly disappeared from the town and gone about his own pursuits, whatever they might be.

Everywhere, among the tall houses on Kinterbury Street or the hovels on Bretonside, the toast was Bess. And she found the very ladies who had been so spiteful in their gossip, competing to have her as their guest.

For weeks after the rescue of the fishermen, her evenings were filled with supper invitations. Again the most presentable of the town's young men were put up for her inspection, sometimes discreetly, sometimes forthrightly, sometimes with a broad and awkward hint.

Bess found herself grow irritable with the attentions of those she did not want to bother with and her inability to do those things she wanted to do.

She tried to talk to some of her hosts of her plan to settle Maravila Island, but met again with frustration. There was interest enough in settlements, but each one's eye turned a different way. Some thought to get a return in one year, from golden cities hidden in the Guyana jungle; some reckoned more shrewdly on a venture in Virginia and its tobacco (if they were not already dealing in smuggled Spanish tobacco). Others had their eyes on cooler lands to the north, on the Kennebec River and Cape Cod, long known to the West Country fishermen. Those who had money to venture, it seemed, had it already earmarked. But they told her cheerfully:

'Your fortune, Mistress Morten, needs no partners.'

That was the trouble, Bess said to herself. Her fortune had a partner, or rather a master, and he would control it for four more long years.

Others soon became impatient, too. Tom and his mates, slowly recovering from their ordeal, began to chafe at their idleness.

'If we'd a ship in trim, and stores, we might make a run for the Banks, late as it is,' said Tom.

But, it was clear that Trant was in no hurry to employ his rescued crews.

Judith and the other wives, occupied with the care of their families, with their spinning and weaving, found their husbands grow more restless by the day. They told Bess frankly:

'When they were away, we did long to have them home. And now they're home, we find them round our feet like children.'

And one added, as her feet and hands flicked busily at the wheel: 'Aye, Mistress Morten's no fool. Let a maid stay free so long as she can.'

Bess nerved herself for another talk with Mordecai Trant. He was as implacable as ever, but now it seemed to Bess that creeping age was adding vagueness to his other irritating ways. She went to speak with him in the counting house, and asked him bluntly when he would let the idle boats sail to Newfoundland.

He shook his head. 'Not this season. 'Tis too late.'

'Not so, Mr Trant. Tom Curnock says 'twould be worth the try, late or no.'

'Tom Curnock proposes, but circumstances dispose otherwise.'

'How so?'

He looked round vaguely and fiddled with his papers. Then looked blankly at her.

'Why may the boats not sail?' she asked.

'We cannot pay for stores,' he said at last.

'Why can we not? There must be the means.'

'While the boats were laid up I moved the money into other ventures. It must not stay idle,' he said, his eyes suddenly gleaming.

'What other ventures?'

'Some is out at interest to other houses. With some I have bought futures in corn.'

'Loans cannot be called in so soon, but our interest in the corn we may sell, may we not?'

He shook his head violently.

'Nay. Next season corn may rise ten shillings the quarter at the least. To sell now would be folly.'

Tom and his mates came to see her. She met them in the courtyard and they sat drinking ale in the sunshine. Bess told them what Trant had said.

'I can do no more, Tom. But be patient. Had I the say, you'd sail for the Banks so oft you'd plead for mercy.'

'Aye, Bess. But 'tis a time to wait. Old Trant grows worse as he grows older.'

'I've other plans, too,' said Bess impulsively, and began to talk to them of Maravila and her dream of a settlement. The fishermen looked at one another, the older shaking their heads, but the younger men listening with keen attention.

'Does the isle have fish?'

'In plenty, though other than cod.'

'Cod we can be without.'

'There'll be land to work for each. Rain and sun in season and no frosts. Two crops a year, and fruit at arm's length on the trees.'

Old Ben Curnock laughed, though his eyes were affectionate.

'Haply the pigs run round roasted with knives stuck in their backs, singing "eat me" as it says in the old song.'

'You'll see, Ben.'

'Nay, Plymouth-born that's me. Plymouth-buried I'll be.'

Impatience in his voice, Tom broke in.

'Aye, but what of now, this season and next? Old Trant's so tyrannical, how do we know he'll let us sail next season? How do we know fish are not cast overboard, and corn taken in in its stead?'

' 'Tis so,' said another man, 'I for one have had enough of sitting on my stool watching my wife earning our bread.'

'True. 'Tis against nature,' said a third.

'When you were absent, your wife's spinning fed your children,' said Bess angrily.

'We'll not forget that, Mistress Morten. But that's done now. We be home and things must alter.'

'No disputing, now, lads,' put in Tom. 'We'll bid thee good day, Bess. Our thanks. 'Tis not thy fault. But men must work.'

They left Bess brooding. Four more years. It wasn't to be borne. She climbed the stairs to the Broad Chamber and sat a while at her favourite place by the window. She found herself running through in her mind the list of young men in the town who, if they thought they had the chance, would come courting. She had but to choose. One whom Trant could not reject, and she'd have charge of her own affairs. Or would she? A husband could soon become more of a tyrant than Trant. Where would she find a man who would leave her free to rule her own?

A knock interrupted her thoughts. A servant brought a letter. She was invited to the Russell house near Tavistock – a masque and ball.

'Bess Morten,' she said to herself. 'Why will the country look upon thee?'

When Judith heard the news, her excitement was free from any irony. 'But Bess, the greatest in the county do go to the Russells'. Thou must have new clothes.' She looked Bess over. 'What thou dost wear, even thy finest, is well enough for the town, but not for the county. Thou must dress to the fashion.'

'Nay, Judith. I yield not. I shall not truss myself in wood and whalebone and walk with a farthingale under my petticoats like a full-rigged mainmast.'

'Oh Bess, thou hast been absent far too long. Ladies of fashion wear the farthingale no more. The latest from France is the verdingale.'

'And what might that be?'

'Why, 'tis like a bolster round the hips. 'Tis called a bum-roll by the vulgar. It leaves thee free before, and lifts up thy skirts behind. 'Tis very cool when one is hot from dancing.'

'God save us, Judith. What next in this world?'

'I hear that up in London the fastest ladies go in pointed doublets, like men, aye and wear their hair short. It's been preached against.'

'Well that will serve to noise it abroad. Judith, my mind's made up. That Spanish dress in black and white...'

'That rag?'

'Find me a needlewoman who will make me the like of that and that will please me very well.'

' 'Tis true it suits thee, with thy...'

'With my complexion? That's thy meaning. Well 'tis not fashionable to be black in the face.

'But, I'll tell thee this, Judith. In Hispaniola, the fairest are the darkest ladies, slaves, as they say, made free by love. When they dress in white, the Spaniards say *mocha en lecha* – a fly in milk.'

'Oh Bess,' said Judith, uncertain whether Bess joked or not.

'Well, I shall go like a fly in milk and let the ladies say what they will.'

' 'Tis what the gentlemen say that counts,' said Judith.

Martin took another view of the invitation. 'There may be men there whose word counts for something in Court, Bess, who can help thee with thy Maravila plans.'

'True, Martin. I will take note.'

In the dancing in the great hall, Bess drew the eyes of everyone, woman or man. Her deep sunburn over the white of her shawl contrasted so sharply with the faces round her, made pale by art, that she was marked out for nods and gestures, even pointing fingers. From across the floor she saw a small group of men look towards her and recognized Ralph Ferrers. He bowed to her, but kept his distance, for which Bess was grateful. Events having transformed Ferrers from half enemy to half business partner, she was uncertain where they might go now. One of her dancing partners, a man quietly and elegantly dressed, began to ask her about her travels.

He showed well-controlled excitement when she described Santo Domingo, Porto Bello and Nombre de Dios and the shipping of gold, silver, indigo, hides, cochineal and other cargoes. But his enthusiasm waned when she warned that the convoys and the new system of fast post ships had made the armadas and flotas less easy to attack.

'They might be attacked before the convoys gathered, might they not, if a secure base might be found, along the coasts or on an isle off-shore?'

'They might. But would the Spaniards leave the base secure? Would they not crush it?'

' 'Tis a risk perhaps worth the taking.'

'I think not,' she said sharply. His face showed his surprise at her tone. 'There is no future in the privateering game. The wealth of the Indies cannot be pillaged any more. It must be worked, by settled farmers.'

He listened attentively while she spoke of Maravila, then he asked her to come with him into another room. A group of men stood talking. They turned.

'Ah, Gilbert Price. The lady, we have not the honour.'

'Mistress Elizabeth Morten of Plymouth!'

'The name we know.'

The men were introduced. Bess heard the names Eliot, Strode, Pym – men to reckon with in the affairs of the county, and in London.

Price had her tell again what she had told him of New Spain and they listened gravely to her plans for Maravila.

'You have a hand-grip on the matter, Mistress Morten,' said one, 'but I fear there is a part of it that will take more than the labour of your farmers.'

'What's that?'

'To get a patent for settlement from the Crown. It will take years, and cost you much, even with friends at Court.'

'True,' said another, 'but 'tis a worthy venture. It deserves our help.'

'Indeed, Mistress Morten. Do you come up to London when your plans are further forward. Mr John Pym and his friends will lend an ear, and perchance open a few doors.'

Bess went home pleased and excited. Now at last things would take shape. She had her plans. She would have friends in London. She had good people to work with her. They would have allies in their settlement. All that she needed now was to take control of her estate.

' 'Tis a big "all", Bess,' said Martin next day when he had listened to her story.

'Aye Martin, I must find a spell to make the years pass swiftly,' she laughed, 'or find me a fitting husband.'

His face grew serious. 'I would thou would'st not jest on that score.'

'Thy pardon, Martin. I did not know my making light of marriage could offend thee.'

' 'Tis nought,' he answered. 'I must go now. I'll ride to Tavistock.'

'Wilt see thy father?'

'Aye,' he said warmly, 'but not for our family's sake.'

'What then?'

'I had not meant to trouble thee with it, Bess. But these past weeks we've found no sale for the yarn or woven cloth. The trade rises and falls like the waves these days. Bess, we must find either work for the men to do or both wives and husbands will be without.'

'Is there ought I can do?'

'If thou could'st find a way to get around old Trant.'

In the midst of all Bess's vexation, came a letter from the Daunceys. Mary wrote: 'Come and be with us for a day or two. The days are fine, the horses fresh, and there are those who seek your company.'

On the first day, she rode with Hugh and Mary and sat and talked with them in the evening. On the second day a servant brought word that they could not ride with her that morning. Would she excuse them?

'Well, I can ride alone,' she said, and calling for her horse to be saddled she walked down to the stables.

In the yard a man on horseback was waiting, dark red hair falling to the shoulders of his rich blue cloak.

It was Ferrers.

Chapter twenty-two

He dismounted, took off his cap and bowed.

'Good morrow, Sir Ralph. I was not told you were here.'

'I came late at night, when folks were abed.'

'And you're to stay?'

'Perchance. It hangs upon the weather and my mood, and . . .'

'And . . .'

'Mistress Morten. We are both deserted by the Daunceys. If you do not dislike company, maybe we might ride together.'

The servant led out Bess's horse and she mounted.

'Why should we not ride together, Sir Ralph?'

They walked their horses out into tree-shaded meadow. When they were a little way from the farm, Bess spoke.

'Let us not chatter of estate management, nor country gossip, nor the fish market, nor even the state of the privateering trade . . .'

'Nay . . .'

'Let us rather get to the matter in hand. You wish to say something to me, Sir Ralph?'

' 'Tis true, though I do not know if you will care to listen.'

'For what you did to rescue my father's men from the corsairs, I owe you at least a hearing.'

'I'm grateful for that.'

They left the meadow and urged their horses up a slope away from the trees. At the top of the hill, looking down over the rolling farm land, they halted.

'Sir Ralph, begin. Say what you will. I'll listen.'

'Mistress Morten. I would marry you.'

'That's short and to the point.'

' 'Tis not a courtship I propose, but a compact, an accord, agreement.'

'A bargain?'

'Aye, that's it. A bargain.'

'As a proposal, it is not flattering, but it is straightforward.'

'Mistress Morten, we have had little to do with one another, though after a fashion, we are kin. My mother was your father's cousin.'

'True. He bought a house from her and I think they had no other dealings. She did not think it a good bargain.'

'She told you that.'

'She did. She told me further that my family, that is my half brother, robbed hers of their just return on a venture.'

'That too is true.'

'And now you wish to have your recompense?'

To her surprise he nodded.

She set her horse trotting along the high ground. He followed her. She increased the pace, and soon they were galloping side by side, the horses and riders well matched. Bess turned and shouted :

'If I were to out distance you, what would you do?'

He shook his head.

'Would you whip me?'

His face coloured darkly. 'I knew it was you and not the groom that day.'

Again Bess was surprised. 'You knew?'

'Of course. Why did you think I lacked the courage to come and see you. I might excuse myself for whipping your groom, but when I guessed 'twas you, how could I come and speak of that?'

Bess slowed down her horse's pace and Ferrers followed suit.

'But after six years we may talk of it,' she said.

'We may.'

'Well, I will not,' said Bess. 'Let's leave the past to care for itself. Let's talk of the future and of your wish to wed me and recoup a family debt from my estate.'

'Mistress Morten, it is no marriage by the rule that I propose to you.'

'Then I will gladly hear you. Marriage by the rule is not for me.'

'It is the talk of Plymouth and no secret, that you would rule your own estate but may not. The terms of your father's will and your stone-faced guardian forbid it.'

' 'Tis so.'

'I'd put your fortune in your hand.'

'And by your husband's right, transfer it into yours.'

'Not so.'

'How then? What sort of husband would you be?'

Ferrers pointed down over the Dauncey lands.

'This is not my life – to spend my days in managing an estate, watching fat yeomen grow fatter at my expense, paying my taxes, serving as magistrate – burden without reward.'

'Your mother does not think this way.'

'I know. She hopes one day I'll tire of the privateering game and turn home to Ancombe.'

'And you'd have my wealth to restore your estate.'

'Nay,' he answered passionately. 'I need your wealth that I shall not return to my estate.'

'How will that suit me then? A husband that uses up my fortune and does nothing to restore his own.'

'I would not use up your fortune. I would have but a fixed sum every year, to follow my own ends. The rest you would dispose.'

'You'd leave me manage my estate and make no interference?'

'I would have nothing but enough to go my way.'

'And you'd claim no other rights over me?'

'I would appear at Stillman Street, you at Ancombe Ferrers, now and then, for the form.'

'Lady Ferrers would take it ill.'

'It would be me you marry, not her.'

'How could I trust that you would keep this bond?'

'There'd be an agreement, properly signed and witnessed between us, but known only to us, to state our rights and freedoms. Beyond that each is free to go as it pleases them.'

'In everything?'

'In everything. Asking no questions. Being told no lies.'

'I do believe you. But what surety shall I have that our bond will be kept?'

'If it is revealed, the marriage will be dissolved. Man and wife may not pledge to stay apart. That's for the form. Else I will not have it common talk that I took a pension from my wife to go and play.'

'And who'll be our secret witnesses?'

'Francis Durmer for my part, perchance Mr Fletcher for yours.'

'Aha, I thought the fine hand of Mr Durmer worked behind this ploy.'

'You take that ill?'

'No. If Francis Durmer has devised it, there'll be advantage in it.'

He looked at her shrewdly, as if sensing he had won her interest.

'What do you say? Shall we make our treaty? And be wed?'

'I'll think upon it.'

'Not too long?'

'Tomorrow I'll return to town. On Friday you will have your answer.'

He put out his hand and gripped hers firmly.

'To the future then?'

'Aye – but not too far.'

Bess rode back into Plymouth divided between excitement

and alarm at her own rashness. She had demanded time to think but she knew well that she intended to accept Ralph Ferrers's offer. At one stroke she would take charge of her fortune and remain in charge of it. Ferrers is a rogue, she thought, and with a rogue I am safer than with an honest man who'll not be content until he rules my life.

Martin had yet to be won for the plan. She invited him into the Broad Chamber that afternoon and offered him a cup of wine.

'Bess, you are about to burst with something. Tell me is it good or bad?'

'Neither and both, Martin.' She told him of Ferrers's proposal quickly and precisely. 'Well, what do you say?'

He looked at her quietly.

'What can I say? Thy mind is fixed, Bess Morten. If I'm not thy witness, thou'lt find another. My counsel thou wilt not take.'

'Still, tell me thy thoughts, Martin.'

'First, I do not trust this Ferrers nor his man Durmer.'

'Neither do I, but there's surety against that.'

'There's no defence against treachery, Bess.' He paused. 'I am sure that when we met the corsair to exchange the hostages, the Rovers saw Ferrers's ship on the move. 'Twas this that made them flee, not a desire to play us false.'

'Thou hast proof of this?'

'None. Therefore I kept it to myself.'

'And . . .'

'This is the more weighty . . .' Martin was silent, then he burst out:

'Bess, thou hast made a bad bargain. It is not thee. I was at one with thee in saying thou would'st not marry a man who sought only thy fortune. But is it better if thou'lt wed only to have it for thyself? Thou cannot love this man . . .'

'God forbid . . .'

'Then how can'st thou wed him?'

'Martin. I cannot wed a man I care for.'

His lips tightened: 'Why not?'

'I love a man I may not have. To love and wed another were treason – the loving, not the wedding.'

'This man that thou would'st have. Does he belong to another then?'

'He belongs to many others.'

'I understand thee not.'

'And I cannot explain. Martin, forgive me, I had not meant to hurt thee. But,' her voice rose, became hard, 'I will be free. I will rule my fortune.'

He got up from the table. 'Aye, but I fear thy fortune will rule thee.'

He walked to the door. 'Mistress Morten. I am your servant. I will witness this agreement. After that give me leave to go and find another employment.'

'Martin!'

But he had gone.

Chapter twenty-three

In the spring of 1610, when Bess was nearly twenty-two, she became Lady Elizabeth Ferrers. She and Ferrers were married in the parish church at Ancombe, crowded with people from port and country. Trant, his face stone-calm as ever, gave Bess away. He had opposed the match strongly but in vain. As Bess had told him, the Ferrerses were a distinguished family, already linked by marriage with the Mortens. Ralph was a grandson of Abraham Combe, a well-known merchant, and of Henry Ferrers, a famous soldier in the county.

'Bess, he is a privateer.'

'So was Hawkins, so was Drake – aye and Mayor Parker.'

So Trant yielded and Bess married Ferrers. For a few days, to satisfy appearances, they stayed at Ancombe Manor. And on the following week they departed, Ferrers to seek letters of marque from the Duke of Savoy, Bess to go back to Stillman Street and her work, which she attacked with a fury of impatience.

On her wedding day, the full Morten fishing fleet (no fisherman could accustom himself to being called a Ferrers man) was at sea. On the strength of her betrothal she had borrowed from a money-lender the funds needed to get the ships away. The interest charged made her wince. But she found that it was a little higher than the interest charged on loans made by Trant from her estate.

' 'Tis a hot market, my lady,' said the money-lender.

' 'Tis a sin to lend at such a rate,' said Bess.

'When folks are mad to borrow money, 'tis more a sin to lend for less; indeed, 'tis beyond the power of man.'

'Would you say it is the work of God, then?'

The money-lender wagged his head, 'What did our Lord say to the servant, who hid his money under a stone?'

Bess went back to Stillman Street and studied her accounts. She dared not lower the rate at which men borrowed from Morten funds, for fear she could not pay the interest on what she had borrowed. Her ships were at sea and so was her money and neither would answer to her call. She felt a sudden need to speak with Martin Fletcher.

But even stronger was the need to know if he was well. She rode over to Tavistock to see Samuel Fletcher. He greeted her sadly. Martin had forbidden him to say where he was.

'I have hurt him sorely.'

'Bess, if thou did'st know how he did love thee.'

Bess bent her head. 'I know, that is the hurt. For I love another.'

'And marry Ferrers? Ah Bess Morten, child. God guide thee through this wilderness.'

Back in Stillman Street, Bess opened the old chest, took out the book of poems where she had hidden the agreement with Ferrers. There were the signatures, including Martin's, and the words... '... she shall without let or hindrance enjoy and have charge of her fortune.'

What was done could not be undone; she must make the fruits of the contract justify the deed. She slipped the document back into the book and replaced it in the chest. From then on she gave herself no rest. No sooner was one task done, when she turned to another. The wool trade had begun to revive after a bad year. Judith and the other women missed Martin's help in the buying and selling so Bess gave a hand, riding round the country to visit the merchants.

When the boats sailed back that autumn, the catch was good, if not abundant. Tom Curnock reported the Banks had been swarming with vessels, a hundred from Devon alone.

'I know not how many more seasons we shall get, Bess,' he said with a touch of anxiety in his voice.

'Then think on Maravila Island.'

Think on Maravila was the refrain to all her private thoughts. In the Broad Chamber, now rarely used for entertainment, the table was piled high with documents, maps, account books, all to do with her project. She calculated a dozen times the funds that she would need to begin the settlement. Each time the figure grew.

And she could not guess what might be the cost of getting Crown approval for her scheme. So far her letters to Gilbert Price in London had brought the answer that the time was not ripe. One thing was sure, though. She must have more money.

That year the price of corn rose twelve shillings a quarter and the purchases that Trant had made paid off handsomely. Bess repaid what she had borrowed and with the rest of the money, bought out Mordecai Trant's share in the business. Trant, now grown feebler, had no opposition to offer. He did not complain for Bess paid generously. Every now and then he would visit her in the counting house, sitting mournfully at a desk and shaking his head while Bess worked.

For form's sake, each second week, she rode over to Ancombe, and appeared in the parish church beside Susannah Ferrers. Bess knew that Susannah was now more hostile to her. The marriage was not as she had planned. But Bess was careful to behave modestly in front of Susannah, now more imperious than ever in her sixties.

On the rare occasions when he came home, Ralph called, for form's sake, at Stillman Street, where his courtesy and arrogant charm won the servants. Bess wondered at the care he gave to his act, but she had no reason to complain and gave him none.

Now and then Francis Durmer would call at Stillman Street to draw his master's funds and then depart for Exeter, Southampton or even London to see to Ralph's affairs. Bess found him still as unlikeable, but a useful man.

He saw to her errands too, carrying out her orders swiftly and without fail. From time to time, Bess found herself talking over business matters with Durmer. His judgements were shrewd but offered with tact. She sensed he studied her affairs closely in his master's interest but so far the attention did her no harm.

Two years passed with alarming speed. Two fishing seasons, two harvests gave good results and solid increase. She went to London to inquire from Gilbert Price how her quest for the Royal Seal on Maravila Settlement was faring.

'Things go slowly,' Price told her. King James had set his face against all colonizing in the Spanish Americas.

'Why should that be? We are at peace with Spain.'

'That is the answer. Now Lord Cecil, our chief minister has died, Count Gondomar, the Spanish Ambassador, carries too much weight at Court. The King will do nought to displease Spain. We must wait for things to change.'

'How long?'

'I cannot say, Lady Ferrers.'

'And my money's spent for nought?'

'There is no other way. Without the King's word no ship may put to sea, much less supply new colonies in the Americas. Sir Walter Raleigh pays a high price. His search for El Dorado has led him to the Tower.'

'This Court's a bottomless pit down which our wealth pours,' said Bess bitterly.

'I beg you, Lady Ferrers. Keep such thoughts for those who know you well.'

Time passed. Bess marked it, not in herself, for work filled her days, but in others. Ben Curnock died, peacefully, content with his family's recovered fortunes. Grandson Tom was now a lively lad, who played on his father's boat and hoped in not too many years to sail in her. Next year, Trant ceased his gloomy weekly visits to the counting house and stayed at home. Bess went to see Trant and his wife now and again. Watching them in their small, walled garden, white-haired and bent, she wondered at their power to thwart her in the past.

Word came from Gilbert Price in London. Count Gondomar had gone from London – in anger it was reported. Royal favour smiled on those who sailed to the Antilles. Patents and charters for settlement in Barbados and Bermuda had been given. Why not Maravila? But new approaches would need more money...

Just as suddenly, the wind changed and blew the other way. Young Prince Charles and the Duke of Buckingham, favourite at Court, were off to Spain to seek a Royal marriage with the Infanta.

'We scarce can further our own concerns, Lady Ferrers, much less look to others',' Gilbert Price told Bess. 'Mr Pym himself is out of favour and may not leave his house.'

'Why's that?'

'He worked too hard in Parliament to aid men with grievances against the Bishops. And he must pay the price. But other men, in lower stations, have fared worse. There's one in Kent, whose ears are cropped, he's flogged, jailed – and robbed of his goods, on a matter of the faith.'

Bess thought suddenly of Martin and his ironic 'crop my ears – they say 'twould make me less ill-favoured', and shuddered. But she was reassured, on her return to Plymouth, to hear from Sam Fletcher that his son was well.

Fletcher had other news. 'Those families from the Church in Holland – those that Martin did help, twelve years ago. They've taken ship to sail to New Plymouth near Cape Cod in New England. They'll make a new home there.'

'They'll have it hard there. Tom Curnock tells me the living's hard in that land.'

'If they get so far, Bess. My news is their vessel's dismasted and they must put into port here.'

'God save us, they'll be in a sorry state. Women and children, too?'

'Near on two hundred.'

'We must help them, Sam. See, I'll go to the port. We'll find them lodgings, while their boat's repaired. They'll need rest and food.'

'True. They had to sell much of their stores to pay their debts before they start. They paid dearly in London even before they started.'

'That's hard. I will not have it so when my people sail for Maravila.'

'Still dreaming of Maravila, Bess?'

'Plans, not dreams, Samuel Fletcher.'

'Bless thee, Bess Morten.'

'Ferrers.'

'Aye, I'd clean forgot.'

When the roughly-repaired ship had sailed for New England, Judith called on Bess.

'I've a message for thee, my lady.'

'Mock not, but give it to me.'

'The women from the ship did say to me "Who was the lady that did help us?" I said which one did they mean, and they replied, "Why she was thin, and somewhat roughly-dressed, though well-spoken – yet thin and greying somewhat in the hair."'

'Who can they mean? They cannot speak of me.'

'How wouldst thou know? I'll wager thou hast not looked in thy glass since thy wedding day.'

'And what use have I for glass? But aside from messages of import, what brings thee here, Mistress Curnock?'

'Bad news from the wool men. All trade's at a standstill. No hope of improvement before next year.'

'Please God the fishing will go well, then.'

'Amen, Bess. I did once say to thee that Maravila was a dream. But now I wonder. To work one year and lose it all the next is hard.'

'Judith, Maravila's no dream. 'Twill come to pass and before too long. A year or two, maybe three and our first settlers will sail.'

B. M

That season on the Banks was poor. Two ships foundered in a storm though most of the men were saved. Things went badly on all sides. But the corn market held up and interest rates rose. Money flowed in. So it went for three years, good and bad treading on each other's heels.

And with the following year came good news. Prince Charles and Buckingham were back from Spain in a rage, insulted by their treatment there. And soon after that came word from London that a Royal patent for Maravila was in preparation. Bess drew her balances once more. It seemed there was enough there to begin.

She bid Tom Curnock go and find a handy ship, 300 tons or so, and set to work herself to buy the stores. After a two months' search, Tom found a sturdy craft that had been used in the West Indies contraband trade. It was called *Hope* and all saw the name as a good omen.

Now Bess began, with some help from Sam Fletcher, to choose her first settlers. They would form the advance party, survey the island and set up a base. Tom, with Judith's consent, had agreed to lead this party. The *Hope* would sail in the spring, Tom would explore the island in the summer and if signs were favourable, return in the autumn to prepare for next year's voyage. The advance party, all single men and in their twenties, save Tom, were half of them fishermen or fisher's sons, half of them farm lads from the country round. With memories of Captain Yarwood's *Bonaventure* in her mind, Bess paid close attention to both quarters and stores.

In the midst of these preparations, when she went home from the port to take a hasty meal, Bess found Samuel Fletcher, his old face strained and worn beneath his white hair, waiting at her door.

'What, Sam, what's amiss? Art ill?'

'Nay, Bess, I'm well. But it's gone ill with Martin.'

He hesitated.

'Wilt thou help him, Bess?'

Chapter twenty-four

'Where is Martin?' Bess asked the old man.

'He lies in a lodging near Custom Quay. He is pursued. If the Bishop's men find him, I fear for his life. Already he is sick.'

'What's his offence?'

'Peddling sermons that the public hangman burned.'

'What may I do for him?'

'If thou could help him leave England, bring him secretly aboard a boat.'

'Take me to where he lies, Sam.' The old man led the way, down Vauxhall Street, then into a narrow alley. At a street door she recognized one of the fisherwives, who pointed up a flight of stairs.

'He sleeps,' she whispered.

'Becky,' said Bess, 'canst thou bid Tom Curnock and Amyas come here. We'll take him aboard the *Hope* tonight. He'll lie safer there.'

Upstairs Martin slept quietly. The well-remembered face was pitifully thin and pale, deep lines beside the mouth. Bess took one hand that lay outside the blanket. She saw red scars on the wrists, and in a flash of memory, touched her own arms.

'Gyves,' she whispered.

'Aye,' said Sam, 'he fled from jail in London.'

Martin's eyes opened, blinked, then a smile slowly smoothed the lines on his face.

'Bess.'

She knelt by the bed and took his shoulders in her arms.

'Martin, rest easy. We will see thee safe aboard a ship tonight.'

'Thou'rt too kind to one that did forsake thee.'

'Not too kind, Martin. Thou must have food, clothes for thy journey.'

'Bess. All I ask is let one of the fishing boats that sail to the Banks take me to Providence Point near Cape Ann in New England. I have good friends there.'

'Martin, that may not be. Thou'lt die. Tom Curnock's told me. It's bleak and bare. Berries and shellfish, nothing more.'

'Prophets lived well on less,' he smiled.

'Martin, our ship, the *Hope*, leaves next week for Maravila Island. Our work of settlement will begin. There thou canst lie in the sun, sleep, grow fat and well-favoured.'

He was silent.

'What is it Martin?'

'Bess to speak will be but to offend and I've done that once too many times.'

'Now if thou tell me not what's wrong, thy offence will be doubled. Speak, Martin.'

He raised himself up, bracing his shoulders on the wall behind the bed.

'Thy Maravila dream has cost thee dear, Bess.'

'What of it?'

'And others too.'

'How so?'

'Thou hast found money for the venture in three ways. Thy fishing fleet, no harm in that. But thou hast bought and sold futures in corn. Each time the harvest's poor, the price goes up, thy coffers fill. Bess, I have travelled round the land. People have starved for want of corn. The name "forestaller" is a hateful thing.'

Bess stared. Her heart grew cold.

Martin went on: 'Thou hast lent money out at interest and the rate is high. In London I met Standish, seeking to borrow for the settlers in New Plymouth. The rate was fifty per cent, Bess.'

'That I have never asked.'

'Aye, thou hast dabbled where others washed their hands.'

'But Martin, I did these things, that poor folk might find a place to make life over again.'

'And beggared more . . . ?' He stopped, 'I have no right to say these things, and ask thy help.'

'No Martin, 'twas I that forced thee to it. But what of of thy friends in Cape Ann? How have they made their way?'

He grimaced: 'Shellfish and berries, borrowing at fifty per cent. But in time they will owe no man and no man will own them.'

She frowned. 'I must go on with what I have to do. But I promise thee I'll deal fairly. Let me once find haven in Maravila and I'll deal no more.'

'Thy Utopia, Bess?'

She got up from the stool. 'Martin, soon Tom and Amyas will come and bear thee on board the *Hope*. Thence we'll say farewell again. But bless thee, Martin Fletcher. God go with thee.'

'And thee, dear Bess.'

Long after Martin had sailed for New England, smuggled aboard a friendly skipper's boat, Bess brooded over their last words. How could she start the Maravila settlement without more money? How could she get more quickly without harm to others? That summer she sold her holdings in the corn below the market price. It gave her little satisfaction. Some reached the people, but the rest, snapped up by middlemen, went into the towns at a higher rate. She turned gladly from the market to attend to the *Hope*, which sailed in the summer with twenty-four settlers on board. Tom Curnock sailed as skipper and young Tom went on his first voyage with her. He was now broad and strong, a younger version of his father but with Judith's dark hair and eyes.

When the *Hope* had sailed, Bess began to see to the raising and fitting out of the main party. This was to be another thirty, including married men. When they had established themselves the women and children would sail. Bess, though more eager to go than anyone, had to hold back. There was too much to arrange – funds, stores, markets for the colony's produce. She made up her mind she would go with the final party. That meant another two years, but it would be worth the wait if she could make sure all was well.

Tom came back in the late autumn, with the *Hope*. He'd left Amyas Littlejohn, his mate, in charge of Maravila and brought back young Tom, protesting loudly at being dragged away. Tom's reports of the ease with which the land would be worked, fish caught, timber felled to make houses, spread round the port. This proved a boon for there had been disputes among the weaving women. Some were keen on the settlement, others were unwilling to go and even more unwilling to let their husbands go ahead.

'We are well suited here, my lady. We have our work. Our men go to the fishing.'

'What if the fish and wool should fail?'

'Why, life doth go up and down. We take the good with the bad, Mistress.'

But though half the women held back, and their husbands with them, their places in the main party were soon filled. And there were still more people from outside the port eager to join the venture. Tom viewed some of the new arrivals with suspicion.

'They're hot to go. But how when they find man must work on Maravila, as in Plymouth?'

'Tom, let them be tried 'ere they are condemned,' said Bess.

The advance party had been well received by the Cimaroons, Tom reported. They had come over from the mainland with gifts of food, goods to trade. 'They would not take coin, but any iron you could give them.'

He brought a message from Matthew. Ba-umba 'like thy brother' was ageing fast and Akenoro led the tribe. The matter of the Talusi's moving was still unresolved. But perhaps the arrival of settlers would strengthen the young chief's hand.

'Aye,' Bess told Tom, 'at all costs none must offend the Cimaroons in any way. Let that be clearly known.'

The main party sailed in the spring, with stores, and half a dozen cannon for the port. A smaller ship, the *Dove*, was chartered to sail along with the *Hope* and bring back swiftly the first crop harvested. With luck the Maravila colony would earn its first return on the market by the autumn. The port was crowded when the two ships sailed. Sam Fletcher, leaning on his stick, was there. So too were Mordecai and Alice Trant, to give a guarded blessing.

'Well, you have had your wish, my lady. Heaven send that it prosper. For after the feast must come reckoning,' said Trant.

The reckoning came that summer. Bess managed to meet the bills with a small margin, by selling two of her fishing vessels, now lying idle since most of their crews had sailed for Maravila.

The *Dove* returned with a small cargo, though not of high quality. Tom wrote that the colonists had made mistakes with their first planting. With the help of the Cimaroons, it was hoped to put right the errors and to get a second harvest. He sent word of stores urgently needed. It was not a long list, but it cost more than Bess had.

A brief message from Matthew told her that Ba-umba had died. 'When may thy old brother – and thy friends – hope to see thee?' he wrote.

Bess had just balanced her accounts after the departure of the *Dove*, when Francis Durmer arrived. When he was announced, Bess struck the counting house table in a fury of frustration.

'I had clean forgot – my pirate husband's dole.'

Durmer entered and bowed low.

'Cannot my lord wait a little while?' she asked.

Durmer shook his head.

'I fear not. Now that the Spanish marriage plans have gone awry, Prince Charles and my lord Buckingham will have war with Spain. Lord Ferrers has letters of marque to impeach the King of Spain in his American possessions.'

'Where will he sail?'

He shrugged.

'South of Porto Rico or Hispaniola. Who can say?'

'May he steer clear of Darien. We want no coat trailing near Maravila. See, I'll raise the money, Mr Durmer. Come back next week.'

Bess went to the money-lender.

'How may I help my lady?'

'Less than you help yourself, I trow. With £200.'

He took her sarcasm in good part and with equal good humour demanded security.

What was there? House? Boats? Coppins' Farm? No, thought Bess, no mortgaging.

'I expect a cargo 'ere the year ends.'

'Better, I hope, than the *Dove* brought into port this summer.'

'You're well informed.'

His eyes twinkled, 'I have an interest.'

'Well, then?'

'Let us not say a loan. I'll buy the cargo in advance.'

'Forestall it?' said Bess and muttered, 'Caught on my own hook.'

'What did my lady say?'

'Nought for your ears. What will your price be?'

'Three hundred pounds.'

' 'Twill be worth twice that.'

'If good. If bad not half so much.'

'Four hundred.'

'Three hundred and fifty.'

The *Dove* came home with a cargo of tobacco and dyewood that sold for £500. Bess gritted her teeth and forgot her exasperation in attending to the colony's needs. More stores were needed and more men. But Bess was advised that Maravila was not yet ready for the families.

The weaving women, whose men had elected to stay in Plymouth, chaffed their workmates.

'I'll wager your men have clean forgot ye and taken some dark maids to wife.'

Judith snorted, 'Our men are not children to be tied to the loom while the wife weaves.'

The winter dragged its way along. Bess had counted on sailing that spring for Maravila. Now she must wait another year. Judith shook her head over Bess's restlessness.

'One would think it were thy man, not mine that lies across the sea. Thou art so hot to go.'

Bess laughed and said nothing.

But next year no *Dove* arrived. At length word came from the Vice-Admiral's men that the ship had been seized by privateers and sailed into a French port. Impulsively Bess set to work to recover the cargo. But soon she found the cost was too much. When she had paid for the crew to be brought home, she had no more to spare. She raised more money by selling Coppins' and looked around for another ship to take the *Dove*'s place. While she searched, came Francis Durmer on his yearly errand. This time Bess told him, 'I fear your master must attend a better time. I'll pay twice over next year.'

'He'll not be pleased,' said Durmer.

'I'll bear his displeasure,' said Bess.

Durmer bowed and left. But something in the cold grey eyes warned her. She redoubled her efforts to find a ship, but when she succeeded still had not enough to fit it out. She sold more of her reduced fleet, but still was short of what she needed.

The money-lender greeted her with his accustomed warmth.

'A pity I'd not sold that last cargo that now lies in France,' said Bess.

He smiled, 'How may I help my lady?'

'I would have eight hundred pounds.'

'I will give you two thousand, my lady.'

Bess stared.

'Eight hundred will not suffice,' he went on.

'You know my own business better than I do myself. But how two thousand?'

'I'll buy the next seven cargoes.'

'That's but the half of what they'd raise.'

'If good, true. But two thousand as a loan, my lady, will cost you more.'

Bess thought a moment.

'I'll do it.'

'My lady.'

The new vessel, some two hundred tons, old and slow but seaworthy and going cheap, was called *The Safe Return*. Bess held her remaining fishing vessels back in port and made up a crew from among their men. She found a skipper seaworthy and going cheap, was called *The Safe Return*. away, bidding the captain make all speed.

But after three months had passed there was no sign of *The Safe Return*. Nor was there any means of learning what had happened. No ships, not even contraband sailers, were sailing for the Spanish Main that year. And no privateers from those waters were expected home.

Now Judith and the other wives became alarmed. 'We must send another ship,' they demanded.

'What shall we send?' asked Bess.

'We've fishing vessels in the port.'

'But have we crew enough? I sent the best men with *The Safe Return*. We have not enough, even with green hands, to man the ship.'

Rebecca, the woman who had sheltered Martin, spoke up.

'Get the ship ready, mistress. We'll ship as green hands.'
'You'd take the men's place?' said Bess.
'Aye,' said Judith, ' 'tis no more than thou hast done.'
Bess got up from her counting house table.
'We'll do't. Come to the port and we'll find the men.'

Before the fishing vessel could be made ready, Bess had a sudden visitor. A sea captain was shown into her counting house one morning. He was a Dutchman, and though he had aged, she recognized him quickly as the man from Middleburg port who had brought her back from Maravila.

'Madam,' he said gravely, 'I've bad news for you from the island.'

'What is it, sir? Make haste and tell me.'

'I came by there last month, to call for water. Sometimes I've traded with your colonists there.'

'Go on – the point,' begged Bess.

'This time I did not land. I saw smoke in the air. The cabins burned on shore and . . .'

'And . . .'

'I saw the Cimaroon canoes draw off to sea.'

Chapter twenty-five

Three days after the Dutch captain's visit, the fishing vessel sailed, crewed by old fishermen, some now past their sailing days, by boys whose fathers were on Maravila, and five of the weaving women. Some in the port who saw them go shook their heads at the voyage, declaring it a crazy venture.

But the news from Maravila met any doubts. The makeshift crew worked like furies to get the ship away. The winds were fair but could not blow hard enough to match the crew's impatience.

What had happened to the men? Were they alive?

Said one wife, 'I know one thing, we did wrong to trust the blackamoors.'

'But wait until we come to Maravila,' Bess told her, 'and we will know the truth.'

'And if my husband's slain, how will truth aid me?' retorted the woman.

'A truce to disputing,' cried Judith, 'get aloft and puff in the sails, if thou hast breath to spare.'

Three weeks' sailing took them through the outer ring of the Indies and five days later the lookout from the mast top cried out 'Land', as Maravila's peak pushed over the horizon. Night fell as they approached and Bess bid the skipper circle the island at good distance. Next day the little ship crept round the coast, all eyes searching shore line and trees for signs of movement. At noon they sighted the headland and made out the shape of the fort at the entrance to the Bay.

'See,' cried a sharp-eyed lad, 'the flag flies – and *The Safe Return*'s at anchor.'

'Aye,' called Bess. 'But, where's the *Hope*?'

'No sign of that,' the lad replied.

'There's men on shore,' shouted an excited woman.

'Count them.'

'I cannot, they run so. A score, maybe more.'

'A score?' echoed the other women.

'There should be fifty at the least,' said Bess. 'Please God the others are elsewhere.'

'Amen,' said an old man who shipped as mate. 'Look, lady, a boat's pulling out.'

Her sails furling, the ship slowly drew in towards the shallower water, while the boat, pushed forward by her sweating crew, flew out to meet her.

'There's Tom,' shrieked Judith, as a broad-shouldered man stood up in the boat. Tom gestured with his arm to starboard, pointing to safe anchorage. Almost before the anchor dropped the small boat was alongside. Tom came on board and three men followed him. Judith and Rebecca rushed forward to embrace their husbands.

'Thank God, thou'rt alive.'

'Aye Judith, we're alive, thank God.' He turned to Bess. 'We did hope for rescue, but did not know how it might be. Our thanks to thee.'

'Thank thy wife and others who pushed me on. Speak Tom, make haste.'

Tom swallowed, 'Nay, I know not how . . .'

'Are our men slain?' cried a woman.

Tom shook his head.

'Nay, praise God, none are slain. Young Arnold Hobbes has drowned by mischance. Herbert Fenton's dead, too, poor lad. He harmed a leg tree-felling, it turned to gangrene and he died. But none are slain, though more than a score have run away.'

'Run away?'

'Aye, Bess, taken the *Hope* and run away.'

The questions round him rose to a shout. Tom turned to Bess. 'Let's go on land. Our cabins are destroyed, but we have shelter and fresh fruit and meat. Better than ship's tack and mouldy cheese. There we can talk. I'll tell you all that's happened.'

Slowly the ship's boat and the one from shore ferried them ashore. The women from the ship saw their husbands again and wept to find them unharmed, though clothes were ragged and faces blackened by the sun. Food was ready and crew and settlers ate beneath a sailcloth awning on the beach. At a distance Bess could see the blackened frameworks of the cabins and sheds.

'Has all been lost?' she asked Tom.

He nodded.

'All's been lost, even the stomach for more work. Some would have sailed for home 'ere now, if there had been a way. But *The Safe Return* stove in her side planks when she came here and she's not fit for sea. As for the *Hope*, she's gone.'

'Aye,' said Amyas, sitting next to Tom, 'the *Hope* is gone, lady.'

'But how, Tom, where?'

'As to where, haply thou'd best ask thy husband.'

'My husband? What devil's work is he up to?' said Bess amazed.

'Well may you ask, my lady,' said Amyas.

'Peace,' said Tom, 'let's have the story straight. We had begun well, and when the extra hands came out and we heard our cargoes had been sold, though at poor price, we thought it would continue better.

'We'd help from the Cimaroons across the water. Twice thy brother came, though he's now old and weak. They showed us what to plant, and helped us harvest. Some of our men would have them stay and work for payment. And some would have the women stay with us, for other rewards. But a young chief, he spoke our tongue, forbade it. So they went away.

'Next year was hard. Some young lads grew discontented. So we had a meeting and resolved that when next a ship came for cargo, those who had no belly for it might go home. Then came *The Safe Return*, with news that seven years' crops were sold beforehand. And at our meeting, one did say, "If we must serve seven years without return, why did we not sign indentures for Virginia." '

Bess suddenly saw the murky below-decks of the *Bonaventure* and heard Ben Moore's indignant voice, 'Seven years, 'tis slavery.'

Tom went on. 'We resolved that those who would might sail back in *The Safe Return* when she was fit for sea. Then came Sir Ralph and his crew in the *Charles*. He claimed stores from us against a debt you owed him.

'I was unwilling he should have stores without word from you. But I suspected he'd take them by force and,' he shrugged, 'we were no match for two score privateers. Then he set up a cabin on the shore,' Tom pointed to the west, 'for his men to refresh themselves. A score of our young men, and more, took a fancy to the way of life. It seemed to bring its recompense more speedily. They told me they'd elected to join the privateering crew. But bold Sir Ralph did not need fresh hands. His crew feared the prize money would grow less. So when he sailed, these young blades, in the night, stole the *Hope* and took her out to sea. They stole what arms we had, as well.'

'And have not returned?' asked Bess.

'They did. They sailed as far as the mainland, stole away a dozen Cimaroon maids from the shore and brought them back. That much they knew of privateering. Then there was quarrelling. Each man would have his maid. So they sailed again leaving the maids on shore.'

Tom breathed deeply.

'The rest's soon told. Two days after came the Cimaroons to

set their womenfolk free. The same young chief I spoke of led them. He told me that they would not harm us for thy sake, Bess, but that the offence would be punished. They put the cabins in flames, burned all we had, leaving only tools. As they sailed from the island, the young chief said – "Have no fear, you'll see us no more."

'Since then every man waits but to leave. I fear your plans have come to nothing, Bess. We tried . . .'

'Aye,' said Bess, 'five hard years we've tried and nought to show.'

The bitterness rose like bile in Bess's throat. She rose and walked away from the others. As she went, she heard a settler say, low voiced, 'Five years – all for my lady's fancy.'

' 'Twas not her fault,' answered Judith, ' 'twas that hound Ferrers.'

'And she's his wife. Where lies the difference?'

Bess walked farther, heard no more but her own angry thoughts. Caught on my own hook, she told herself, then heard again her own argument with Martin : 'A bad bargain, Bess.'

Well, she would rescue what she could. She turned and walked back to the others. They made way for her silently and she stood under the awning and listened to the waves playing on the shore. She'd heard that sound before on Maravila, but that was long ago. Turning to the men and women she began to speak.

'For all you've suffered, I crave pardon. I did entice you to leave home. 'Tis mine the blame. But once back in Plymouth, I'll try to help you all.'

'Nay, Mistress,' called an old man, 'there's two fishing vessels left. Better we put them in service. Let each earn his bread as we've done before.'

'Aye,' said Judith, 'we'll to our wheels and looms again,' she paused, 'save those who'll ship as sailors.'

Said Tom, 'The sooner we are fit to sail, the better. There

are Spanish ships in the offing. God save us all if they take us.'

He looked up at the afternoon sky, ' 'Twill soon be dark. But we have shelter for the night. Tomorrow we'll begin to work.'

Amid the lengthening evening shadows the settlers made ready to sleep. Now uncertainties were over, all were cheerful. Men and women gathered round fires on the shore. Someone began to sing. Bess wandered down towards the water where the surf line broke white along the sand and looked towards the distant coast. Who would be there now? Now the Talusi were gone. But what of Matthew? Was he alive?

Something splashed in the water out in the bay, like a fish breaking the surface. The splash came again, and again, now regularly. Bess strained her eyes towards movement and sound. It was a boat. The sound came nearer, she saw the white sheen of broken water round the boat's dark shape. At thirty yards from the shore she recognized it in the fading light. It was a Cimaroon outrigger and in it she could see some half a dozen men, rhythmically paddling.

She ran to the water's edge, calling a greeting. Back came a deep answering call. The canoe grounded and a dark figure rose and stepped on shore. Coming closer, he peered into her face. It was a man her own age, and his face was familiar to her. He knew her.

'Bess,' he gripped her arm. 'Mattu – he dies.'

Chapter twenty-six

Matthew dies. The words sank slowly into her mind. Why should she marvel? Matthew was an old man. But he was her brother. She was not ready for him to die.

'Where does he lie?'

'In the old town.'

'And the people?'

'Gone away.'

A question rose to her lips but she did not speak it. The hunter spoke again.

'Morning. We shall wait here.'

She nodded and the canoe pulled away from the shore, swiftly melting into the dusk. Bess turned; Tom and Judith stood near her on the beach. Behind them was Amyas, cutlass in hand.

'You heard.'

'Aye,' said Judith, 'we saw the blackamoors. We feared for thee.'

'Have no fear. Tomorrow I must go to my brother.'

Tom spoke, 'Bess, what if this be a plot to take thee hostage?'

'I'll take that chance.'

They began to climb the beach to the shelters.

'How long will you need to get the ship ready to sail, Tom?'

'Ten days. No more. Longer we may not stay. If Spanish ships are in these waters and they come on us, all's lost.'

'Sail then in ten days. I will return. If not, then sail.'

'But,' protested Tom.

'Sail,' commanded Bess. 'Two score lives and more shall not be hazarded against one. See, Tom, get me a light. We'll send to the ship for paper. I'll give thee letters for Sam Fletcher. If I do not return, thou and the others shall have the ship. Sam shall sell the house and all and so divide what's there.'

'What of thy husband?' asked Judith.

'The devil will take care of his own,' said Bess.

'But may he not prevent thee, by law?'

Bess laughed harshly, 'In the old chest in our Broad Chamber is a paper that will hit him amidships if he tries. Come, there's much to do.'

When morning came, the others crowded to the shore as the canoe glided in.

'Remember, Tom. If I come not, make speed and sail for Plymouth.'

'Aye, Bess. God protect thee.'

'Amen,' said the others.

Bess climbed aboard and the men raised their paddles.

'God speed,' came the call from the shore.

The paddles struck down. The water foamed and they drew away. Beyond the headland, sail was raised and the canoe flew over a glass-calm sea. Bess looked once more at Maravila as the shores and woods blurred in the distance and had the feeling of a final farewell.

Towards evening the canoe grounded on the well-remembered shore. Little had changed there, but the beach was now silent and empty. The path from the sand up through the trees was beginning to narrow as undergrowth crept in. And at the head of the track the silence of the empty huts of the town was strange and fearful.

'Come,' said the hunter.

A single fire burned in the corner of the square, outside Matthew's hut. Bess ran towards it. One wall had been removed, leaving it open to the warm night air. A woman sat and stirred the embers.

They flickered suddenly and she saw the bed of branches and Matthew lying there on the covering of hides, brown wrinkled face amid straggling white hair.

'Matthew,' she called and tumbled on her knees at the head of the couch. His eyes opened.

'Ah, Bess. Thou'rt late in coming. The years have beaten us in the race.'

'Matthew . . .'

He smiled faintly. 'Weep not, Bess. 'Tis easy for me. Or dost thou weep for Maravila and thy dreams?'

'Oh Matthew, all is gone. And 'twas my fault. I've failed.'

'Hush, sister. Thou hast ventured.'

'It is my fault, but I would not be ruled . . .'

'Praise God for that, sister. Never be ruled. Too many stand ready to rule if thou submit.'

'Nay, I meant if I had been less rash.'

'Bess, I would not have thee other. Thou hast been my joy. In thee is nothing mean. What thou hast had, thou gavest freely.'

'But nought is left. Maravila's gone. My people sail back home. No ease for them. Utopia's a dream again. Say Matthew, is it truly nowhere? Never?'

'Nowhere is nowhere, never will never come. I do believe men still will strive.'

Bess suddenly thought of Martin on the bleak shores of New England.

'Aye, Matthew, berries and shellfish.'

'Dost ramble, Bess? 'Twill not do. 'Tis me that's old.'

'What may I do now?' she said.

'May do, must do.' He thought a while. 'Good Sir Thomas More did say, if I remember right – even if thou canst not rule the storm, forsake not the ship.'

She bent her head to his and kissed him. He whispered.

'Sleep now, Bess. Joy cometh in the morning.'

Bess found shelter in a nearby hut, where the hunters had thrown down leaves and grass for a bed. She slept heavily and woke when the sun was high. She heard voices. Someone called clearly in English.

'Bess, why sleep so long? The sun is up.'

She leapt up, pulled her hair from her eyes, straightened her crumpled clothes and ran into the open. On a log by the fire outside Matthew's hut, sat a man, his dark, close-curled hair tinged with grey, but his naked chest still hard-muscled and the dark, well-remembered face gently smiling.

'Akenoro!' He rose and met her as she ran and caught her against him until the breath left her body.

'How . . . ?'

'I came back to be with Matthew, when my people left. They could well spare me. My brothers lead them on. Our watchers saw your ship come to the island. We sent for you. Art wroth with me?'

'Why should I be?'

'That we did burn thy people's homes?'

'Their lives were spared. And now they'll sail to England. 'Twas not thy fault, or theirs. The blame lies elsewhere. But we'll forget that now. I had not hoped to see thee.'

'Nor I thee.'

'How long wilt thou stay?' Both spoke together and laughed.

Bess said, 'Our ship sails in ten days.'

'Then we have time. Let's eat. And then . . . we've horses.'

They rode in the woods, swam from the headland, lay on the sands. In the evening they sat with Matthew, whose half-open eyes showed his pleasure at the sight of them, though he spoke little. When he slept again, they wandered away, built a fire on the sand and saw the moon rise.

'So it was on Maravila, that time,' he said.

'Aye, that's past and done.'

'Not all,' she said, turning to him. 'We are here.'

'True, we are here and well may the world go lost,' he answered.

Five golden days passed. Bess felt her whole self fill with contentment. Not all was lost. She had earned some reward. The sun shone on her and the shadows retreated to the edge of her thoughts. On the sixth day, Matthew died in his sleep. Bess found him in the morning, hands folded on his chest, face gentle in repose, as if a word or a touch would wake him.

From his few belongings, Bess and Akenoro took faded clothes he had not worn for many years and dressed his body. Then with the aid of the hunters, they carried Matthew up the hill to a clear space overlooking the sea. They buried him with care and covered the grave with heavy rocks. While the men stood by Bess said a prayer, and taking a knife scratched in the stone at Matthew's head:

'Matthew Morten. Born 1549? Died 15 March, 1628.
At rest.'

When they returned to the town, Akenoro went into Matthew's hut and came back carrying a bundle wrapped in cow hide. He opened it. Three things lay there. A Spanish sword, a faded Bible with a broken clasp and a necklace of stones that flashed in the sun.

'Matthew told me that you should have these.' He raised the necklace.

'His one vanity. He took it on a raid and put it round Kulokela's neck. Then, when she died, he hid it away. So now, you take them.'

That night as they lay beneath the trees, Akenoro said urgently:

'Bess, why must thou leave? Your people, my people may go on without us. Let us stay here.'

Bess sat up and gazed out on the sea.

'Matthew told me what Sir Thomas More did say.'

'Aye, good Sir Thomas.'
'If thou rule not the storm, forsake not the ship.'
'And thy ship sails eastward.'
'Aye, Akenoro, and thine west.'
'Then let's pledge our love at least.'
'I have a pledge of thee, Akenoro.'
'What's that?'
'Thou must know.'
He laughed in the darkness.

At dawn as they came back into the clearing a hunter ran in from the trees, shouting.

'A boat, a boat.'
'It must be my people, come for me,' said Bess.
'No, no, fly!' shouted the hunter.
'Get the horses,' called Akenoro.

They were barely mounted when a line of armed men burst through the trees from the shore. The morning sun shone on musket barrels.

As the volley crashed across the clearing, Bess threw herself from the horse. As she rolled on the ground she saw two things quite clearly.

She saw Akenoro fall and she saw the face of Ralph Ferrers above her.

Chapter twenty-seven

A fever of madness closed Bess in and cloaked the horror of what she had seen. She lay in her own nightmare world, peopled by fantasy figures that rode and ran and swam and climbed, struggled, fought and struck each other down.

Then it seemed that she woke from one dream into another. A ship heaved beneath her, a lantern swayed, shadows danced on timber beams. Ferrers's face appeared, his voice saying, 'rescue, hostage', and she heard her own crazy laughter; then she saw the face of Durmer, calm and cold. At last both vanished and Bess returned into her inner dream.

She saw Ben Moore and Sir Walter walk an endless road, a girl leap on to the deck of a ship crying 'to the end of the world', a black horseman with a lance, on a wild prancing pony, a rider who struck with a whip and cried mockingly 'your pardon, lady'. Then men at a table bowing to a woman in Spanish lace, and murmuring 'flota', 'armada', 'gold'. And all the figures rose and rushed towards her, crying 'gold, gold, gold'. But a lean brown man swung at them with a sword and they disappeared.

She woke again in a room where sunlight struggled through dusty hangings, and saw an old woman, straight and stiff with a cold proud face. The lips moved, asking questions, but she could not hear them.

Then with a sudden clarity, she heard her own voice cry: ' 'Tis true. I am with child, my lady.'

So once more into her world of dreams. But quietly now,

down a road that gleamed in the darkness. She rode amid a crowd of people young and old, who jostled, joked and chattered. One, in a patched brown jacket, called 'berries and shellfish, good people, think on that, berries and shellfish,' and the crowd laughed. Then she was fully awake in a room she vaguely knew, a room whose window overlooke garden.

A pink-cheeked young woman sat beside her bed.

'What is thy name?'

'Nell, my lady.'

'What is this place, Nell?'

The girl looked puzzled.

'Why Ancombe Manor, my lady.'

'Aye, so 'tis. Then prithee Nell, get my clothes and bid them bring my horse. I must to Plymouth, in haste.'

'But, my lady.'

'Go Nell, and make haste.'

Bess put her feet on the floor and stood up. She looked down at her body. 'That shift's a strange one. When did I buy that?' she mused.

'And this body's not my own.'

A slow hot pulse of nausea beat up through her body. A mist came between her eyes and the room. She felt someone help her back to bed. Then her vision cleared and she saw Ralph's mother, tall and pale.

'Is it true you are with child?'

'Who said so?' asked Bess carelessly.

'You said so.'

'Well, then, it must be true,' said Bess and under the bed covers slowly she placed her hands over her belly. She thought: 'Does it grow within me? 'Tis passing strange. It grows 'an I will it or not,' and she laughed.

'In high humour, my lady?' said Susannah grimly.

' 'Tis true. I shall have a child.'

'And is it Ralph's?'

'Tut, my lady, what a question.' Bess felt light-hearted.

Susannah went out.

She returned with a doctor who looked Bess over, turned to Susannah and said: 'In body sound, but in her wits . . . I fear.'

Bess thought to herself, 'They speak as though they think I know not what they say.' She cleared her throat.

'My wits are sound. I'll have the maid bring my clothes and go to Plymouth and my counting house. I have not been there of late and there is much to do.'

The doctor shook his head.

' 'Tis sometimes so, when woman is with child. But, haply it will pass.'

He left the room with Susannah. Bess called to Nell.

'My clothes.'

'My lady says you shall stay abed, madam.' The girl came closer. 'You must rest. It has been hard for you.'

'What has been hard, Nell?'

The girl shook her head. Bess grasped her arm and demanded: 'What has been hard?'

'My lady. Sir Ralph did find you captive in New Spain, freed you from savages, brought you home.'

'When was this?' said Bess dully.

'Two months since, my lady. You would not wake. We feared for your life and . . .'

'My reason, eh?'

The girl nodded. Bess said distantly, 'My – reason – is – returned.'

The girl ran from the room, calling: 'My lady has fainted away.'

Bess closed her eyes to shut out the light and set her mind grimly to recall all that had happened. Now she had it. Maravila and the ship – Matthew – and Akenoro. Yes, Akenoro. Now she'd found it. Now the pain could come back and settle in her heart.

She opened her eyes again. Now the room was clearer.

The girl came back with damp cloths to cool Bess's forehead.

'Nay, 'tis over,' she said firmly. 'Where's my husband?'

'He waits outside the room.'

'Bid him come in.'

Ferrers strode in, still cloaked for riding. This was the man she knew best, handsome face, insolent eyes.

'You have forgot your whip, my lord.'

'And you made sport and played at madness,' he replied. 'You foxed the doctor and my mother.'

'But you and I, Sir Ralph, shall play at telling truth.'

'It would be best.'

'Then you shall begin. Did you slay the men you found me with?'

'Every one. We'd need to rescue you. If we had waited they'd have fled.'

'Aye, like the doomed corsairs. Strike first and then inquire of the dead, eh, Sir Ralph?'

'We rescued you alive.'

'Now, what of my people from the island?'

'All safe home, a month since.'

'I must go and see them.'

'I think you'll go not to Plymouth for a while.' He smiled grimly. 'One who's to bear a child must be cared for.'

'I must attend to my affairs.'

He laughed. 'They're attended to. By good fortune I came home in time, before your fishermen had seized our boats.'

'*Our* boats?'

'Aye, I've taken them in payment for your debts to me. They're safe outside the port. The house in Stillman Street's another matter. That old fool Fletcher did impeach me in the courts.'

'Thank God for that.'

'But not before I'd searched the house and made an

inventory of my wife's goods. Some I removed for safer keeping.' He held up a piece of paper.

'The contract, my copy.'

'Aye, the contract.'

'You had no right to take it from my house.'

' 'Twas by mischance I found it,' he said mockingly, 'I found it in a book of poems that had my mother's name on.'

She reached out a hand and tried to snatch the paper. He lifted it lightly away and from his pocket took out another document. 'Here's its fellow.'

He called the maid. 'Bring a lighted candle.'

Bess struggled from the bed. He pushed her back as the maid entered.

'Our contract is void. You failed to keep your part,' he smiled at his own word play. 'Apart from that, now we're to have an heir, our marriage is on another footing – as God intended.'

She stared at him, amazed. 'You'll acknowledge the child?'

He shook his head. 'I've a better plan. There is a maid in Ancombe, who's with child by me. There's hardly a month between your child and hers. We'll make a fair exchange. She'll be well paid, and who will be the wiser? Ancombe Ferrers will be inherited and mother will be well pleased. While I'm on voyage, you may busy yourself with my affairs, as a good wife.'

'You are a fool, Ralph Ferrers. This child of mine cannot be exchanged.'

He looked puzzled. 'Why, will he have his father's mark on him?'

'He will.'

He grew curious. 'Which of your bold fishers is the father? Curnock? Or was it Fletcher? No matter. We'll see to that in seven months time. Now, to dissolve our contract.'

He held one paper to the flames. It blackened. Then the other shrivelled.

'What of your witnesses, Ferrers?'

'Durmer is my man. His ears, eyes, mouth and hands are at my service.'

'What of Martin Fletcher?'

'He's in New England, shivering in righteousness.'

'He could return.'

He rose and crushed the ashes between his fingers, brushed them from his hands.

'I'll get you pen and paper. You can write him. He'll return. He's a loyal man. And the Bishop's Pursuivant will await him with open arms.'

Ferrers saw her shudder, smiled and left the room.

In a few days Bess was strong enough to walk about. The bedroom door stood open, but across a passage, another door was locked. The window was barred. Lady Ferrers was intended to stay in her husband's room.

Nell brought her books to read and chatted with her each day. After some weeks, the girl said impulsively, 'Your babe begins to show, my lady.'

Bess looked at the high curve under her breasts and said, 'What do folk say of me, Nell?'

'In Ancombe it is said you are with child and not too soon. But then again, not too late, praise God.'

'Do you go to Plymouth, Nell?'

'But rarely, madam.'

'But, say to the ferry?'

'Now and then, to meet my sister.'

'Wouldst take a note? 'Tis but to my maid there, Judith Curnock, that she may send some things to me from my house.'

'I'll do it, my lady.'

Next day Nell did not come. In her place another older woman sat by the door.

'Where's Nell?' asked Bess.

'Gone away, my lady.'

'Go call Sir Ralph.'

Ferrers came in a moment later.

'You have not harmed that maid?'

'She has been sent away.'

'Then let me have my letter back.'

'I cannot. The ferryman took it.'

Bess breathed slowly. He raised his eyebrows. ' 'Tis pity it cannot be delivered.'

'What do you mean?'

'I had forgot to tell you. The fishing boats are sold. Curnock and his mates bought them. The price was not high but no one else in the port would bid. So I let them go.'

He paused.

'And Curnock and his good wife and some others sailed from the port, last week, bound for Newfoundland, I'm told.'

Chapter twenty-eight

The news left Bess in a black mood of helplessness. To match her mood, the sky outside her barred window turned to grey and the leaves in the garden to autumn brown.

As the child inside her grew and weighed lower in the cradle of her hips, so her body grew leaner, her face thinner. She saw it briefly in the glass, bony and witch-like, framed in wisps of black-grey hair. As she moved about the room, she felt the baby shift, its weight pressing on a nerve, and she winced. Her step grew heavier.

She had one hope – Sam Fletcher. If he knew of her real plight and he could reach one of the Plymouth council men, or even Gilbert Price with his powerful friends in London, a means might be found to release her. Bess tried to coax her maid to take a letter, but in vain. In desperation she wrote another and threw it from her window. She heard no more for a week.

Ferrers brought it back and placed it on the table by her bed. He said briefly.

'Old Fletcher died last month.'

Bess turned her head away.

'But 'ere he died, he so tied up your affairs in court that I shall have the devil's job to unwind them.'

'That's a work to suit you,' she answered.

Later that month she had another idea. She demanded more books to read. Ancombe Manor's stock was soon read through.

'We'll ask the priest,' said Ferrers.

'That man's a blockhead. Can you not send to St Andrew's in Plymouth and beg books of the minister there?'

He thought a moment.

'Write a list. Someone shall take it. Someone I can depend on.'

Five minutes after, Durmer came into the room. His bow was as formal as ever, his eyes cool and watchful. He took the list and left with a bow. That afternoon he brought the books.

'The minister bids you well and wishes you a safe confinement, my lady.'

'Safe confinement's all I have, Mr Durmer.'

He appeared not to notice her irony.

'What news of Plymouth?' A gleam of interest appeared in the grey eyes.

'Turmoil in the town. Sailors pressed for service in the Rochelle expedition declined the honour. They were locked in the Guildhall and the leaders were to be hanged. But the men broke out, tore down the gallows and ran away.'

'The war's not to their taste.'

'With men that will not fight and masters that will not pay taxes, King Charles has his hands full.'

'When war's declared and taxes levied without consent, who can expect else? King James sowed the wind. His son reaps the whirlwind,' said Bess.

'There's more than votes and taxes now, my lady. Sir John Eliot, Mr Pym and others known to you, are deep into some plot in Parliament. They play for high stakes. Someone will lose all, King or Commons.'

'And what think you, Mr Durmer?'

'Nought, madam, save this. They began by seeking to save their pockets. Now they want more – they want the realm.'

'And you, Mr Durmer, go no further than your pocket directs?'

'As my lady pleases,' he bowed and left the room.

When Bess had read the books, or pretended to, she wrote a letter to the Minister of St Andrew's and slipped it inside a volume. When Durmer returned from Plymouth with fresh books, he handed the letter back to her unopened, without a word.

The days grew colder. A fire was made up in the grate of the bedroom, but it smoked and spluttered without giving warmth. Bess put on extra clothes and roamed the room beating her hands together. She felt the child thump at her side.

'Thou'd be out, eh? Take my counsel. Stay inside where 'tis warm. Thy mother's fit to perish here outside.'

December came and the first snows. The sky lightened, outside a white edge appeared on the window sill and the air grew a little warmer.

One day as she sat and talked to Durmer, Ferrers came into the room, grinning like some mischievous boy.

'The child's born. It's a boy.'

She glanced at Durmer who stood near the door. Ferrers said easily, 'Oh, Durmer's in on all my schemes. He's made many of them.' He turned again to Bess.

'I've had the boy brought into the house with his mother. No one else knows. They'll be to hand when your whelp's born. It will be done in a flash. My son will be yours and Sir Ralph and Lady Ferrers have an heir to show the tenants.'

'You'll not change those babies.'

He turned on her, eyes suddenly hostile.

'Twice you said so, madam. What's your meaning?'

He came near her, seized her wrist painfully.

'Say, who is the father? Who is it?' he shouted, his face suddenly crimson with rage.

She shook her head.

'Well, all's one to me. Change or not, my child shall be yours. As to the other brat – girl or boy, we'll find another way.'

Bess felt a sudden pain of fear at her heart.

'What do you mean?'

He laughed and left the room.

'My lady?'

Bess turned, alarmed at the voice. She had forgotten Durmer stood in the room. He carefully closed the door and came near her. He spoke low.

'Madam, if you would save your child, you must leave the house.'

'I have sought to leave, Mr Durmer, and you know it.'

'I know it, madam, but with my help you may do so.'

She stared at him. The grey eyes looked evenly back.

'Lady Ferrers. I know you do not care for me. But you have never wronged me. I have been used courteously by you. Only those who serve know what these things mean, madam.'

'Go on, Mr Durmer.'

'I know the father of your child's no Devon fisherman, nor preaching weaver. He is a chief among his own people, is he not?'

'How did you know?' Bess gasped.

'My lady. You are no weakling. Why should you fall and rave and lie in fever when the Cimaroon was slain? I know these signs.'

'But your master does not.'

'There is much he does not know. My employment is to know better than he.'

'Ferrers has the will, Durmer points the way,' murmured Bess.

'Aye, Mistress Dauncey's words. But 'tis not true. I do not lead him on. I hold him back.'

'Aye, when he goes beyond the sound interest, eh?'

'I don't deny it. When he is mad to do a thing, he'll do it, heedless of advantage or return.'

'Or profit.'

'Aye, my lady, and I see no profit in murdering your child.'

A spasm of pain raced through Bess's body and the child inside her leapt. She clutched at the chair back.

'Shall I call your maid, my lady?'

'Nay Durmer, say on. What profit is there in saving my child? It would cost you dear.'

'I know, Madam. I would have payment. Among the bundle brought back from Darien is a necklace.'

'Your eyes are sharp.'

'Sharper than most, else had another robbed you already. That necklace will be my payment if I bring you safe to Plymouth.'

'It was a gift...' she said half to herself.

'Your child's life...'

'How do I know you'll not betray me.'

'Madam, your escape will be mine also. You take the bundle. Give me the necklace when you are safe, and I'll away.'

'Why do you not take the necklace now and begone? I can't prevent it.'

He burst out with sudden passion. 'I will not have a new-born child's death on my hands.'

Bess looked at him in silence a moment.

'Mr Durmer, I am in your hands.'

'Madam, be ready dressed tonight. Lie in your bed. Wait till you see me call the servant away. Go by the door across the passage, which I'll leave open. I will be there. That's all.'

Bess lay in the dark under a single cover. She heard whispering, saw the maid get up and go from the room, leaving the door ajar.

Her body dragged as she stood up and tiptoed awkwardly across the room. Her head sang with excitement and her body was alive with warmth and movement, nerves twitching. Outside the frosty night air struck her in the face. The ground was white and iron-hard. Someone stepped behind her, throwing a cloak about her shoulders, took her arm and led her along a wall in shadow.

'We must make haste. I've horses in the field beyond.'

Bess stumbled in the frozen, rutted yard and nearly fell. Durmer held her up and urged her on in one movement. They skidded on ice and tripped on frosted clumps of grass and clods of earth.

'For charity's sake, Mr Durmer. I can't go faster.'

'Wait by the hedge. I'll bring the horses,' he whispered.

The darker shapes of the horses loomed up in the dark. A sudden rolling spasm swept through Bess as if each muscle clenched like a fist and then let go.

'Here, madam. Mount now.'

Bess was almost in the saddle, her swollen body lopsided, when dogs barked and lights went on in the house.

'We're discovered,' she said.

'Be still and wait,' commanded Durmer.

From the house came shouting, curses, the sound of horses being led out. Lights showed beyond the stable wall. Men mounted. One, two, three horses galloped down the track into the night.

'Come, madam, let's away.'

'Which way? They're on the Plymouth road.'

'I know not, madam. But away we must.'

Bess had an inspiration.

'We'll ride north to the Daunceys. 'Tis the only hope.'

They set off. Bess rode as in a trance, now bending forward as another spasm took her body, now leaning back to ease her cramped muscles. Durmer took her reins and led her horse along, down narrow rutted lanes, on narrower tracks as the ground rose higher, and then on open grassland. The moon came up and filled the frosty world with light.

'Let me get down, Mr Durmer.'

They dismounted. She seized his arm and bowed over it as her whole belly now clenched and unclenched like a fist.

'Are you in pain, my lady?'

'Nay, thank God, no pain, Mr Durmer. But I cannot command my limbs. My body does its work without me.'

'Can you mount again? 'Tis three miles more.'

'You'll need to lift me, Mr Durmer.'

She struggled, Durmer heaved and the slow rocking heaving ride began again. Her body began to numb, the skin prickled with the cold. But inside she was strenuously alive. Her heart raced. She groaned.

Durmer turned.

' 'Tis but me, Mr Durmer. My time's near. I must get down.'

'But a little way madam. The manor is down there in the hollow.'

'Nay, I cannot have my child on horseback, sir.' Bess slid down.

'Help me to that barn.'

Twice they slipped in the grass, but struggled up again. Twice they stopped to let Bess find her breath. Her lungs pumped more powerfully and faster, her breath reached from the depths inside her, sighed in her mouth.

Durmer flung open the barn door. Bess took half a dozen paces and fell in the piled hay. She lay back and let each spasm of her muscles ride through her like a wave.

'Pray leave the door open. 'Twill soon be dawn. Meanwhile moonlight's enough for my work.'

Durmer stood still. Bess remembered.

'Nay – here – take your payment. The – bundle's at – my saddle.'

He went out and Bess waited, clutching on her skirts as the waves of strain and release passed after one another down her body. The straining movement flung up her clothes. Durmer stood in the doorway.

'I have the jewel. The sword and Bible are here,' he stooped to lay them at her side. As another tremor shook her body, she seized on his arm and held fast.

'Nay – help – me.'

'How may I?'

Bess heard a note of alarm in his voice.

'Nay, Mr Durmer. I shall bear it like a woman. Do you bear it like a man. Go get help, bring water. I'll do the rest.'

Durmer left her again.

When the child came, Bess, absorbed in her body's work, did not hear hoofbeats on the ground outside.

She was cradling her slippery brown boy to her breast when a man strode in through the barn doorway.

It was Ferrers.

Chapter twenty-nine

The dawn light through the doorway showed Ferrers's face clearly, but it was some seconds before he saw Bess crouched over her baby in the hay. His cheeks were red-purple with cold, his jaw clamped tight, a small muscle flickering beside his mouth. He did not see Durmer enter the barn.

Ferrers spoke at last.

'You were right, my lady. The child hath his father's mark on him. He's not for exchange.'

Bess folded the edge of her cloak more tightly round the child at her breast. Her voice was weak but level.

'Now that you know sir, I beg you depart to your own house and let me go my way in peace.'

'Depart?' Ferrers's voice was high pitched. 'You shall return to Ancombe. And the brat . . .' He took a step forward, metal shone in his hand.

'By Christ, no,' shouted Durmer and flung himself forward, meeting Ferrers's lunge, knife in hand. A half shriek came from his mouth Ferrers's knife blade went home. His knees bent, his body arched and he slid into the hay at Bess's feet.

'God see thee safe in hell, Ferrers,' he gasped and lay still.

Ferrers in blind rage kicked out at Durmer's body. Curses bubbled from his lips.

'Hold, Ralph,' the command came from the barn door. Hugh Dauncey, in shirt sleeves, sword drawn, stood there. 'Compound not thy crime with blasphemy.' Behind Hugh, Bess could see the shocked faces of farm servants. Dauncey turned.

215

'Help up my lady Ferrers to my sister's room. Take care, bear gently. And two of you bear out Durmer's corpse. Aye, and send a lad for the sheriff's men. Ralph, put down thy blade.'

They lifted Bess and brought her into the manor house.

Mary, pale and alarmed, still dressed in her night clothes, had water heated. Mother and child were washed and put to rest. The midwife, called from the village, looked them over in some surprise, pronounced them well. Bess drifted off to sleep. She woke near noon, and refusing Mary's offer to bring in a wet nurse, gave the child milk and slept again, this time waking when the baby cried. She sat up and took him from the crib that had been placed by the bed. Mary came in. 'It snows again. How does my lady and her child?'

'My lady and her son,' corrected Bess. 'We do well, thanks to our friends.'

'How do you find him?' she asked Mary.

'He's well-favoured,' said Mary.

'He hath his father's nose,' said Bess, 'and straighter than mine.'

'He's well-favoured,' said Mary.

'Thou dost not ask how I did come by him.'

'Bess, for my sins, I know how ladies come by babies. What I do know, too, is that the child's not Ralph's.'

She sat down by the bed.

'Bess, I am thy friend. Ralph is a man of violence. But hast thou not provoked his rage?'

'Aye, that I have, Mary. What happened in the barn today's another chapter in a long and secret story.'

Mary's face was serious.

'Adultery's a sin.'

'True, Mary, but the least of mine. Had I not pride beyond the needs of one mortal, all this had not happened. Save him,' she rubbed her cheek against the dark down on the baby's head.

'For this pledge of love I'd turn back the book and begin again.'

'There's much we do not know . . .' began Mary.

'Aye, and when thy Hugh comes home, I'll tell you all. I cannot bear to tell it twice.'

That evening Hugh rode home and the three ate supper in the room where Bess lay. The brown boy slept in his crib while Bess told her story in a low voice.

'A strange tale, Bess,' said Hugh, 'I cannot find it in me to pass judgement on it, save to say this – thou hast ventured perilously. And I fear thy troubles are not at an end.'

'How so?' asked Mary anxiously.

'Today I was with Ralph before the sheriff. Ralph's two men will swear that Durmer drew first. In Durmer's pocket a jewel was found, that Ralph said was his wife's. If a case should come to trial, none will accuse a gentleman for slaying a servant who kidnapped and robbed his own lord's wife and would have slain her husband.'

'That's monstrous untruth,' protested Bess. 'I would speak up for Durmer.'

'Bess,' said Hugh. 'Durmer's beyond help. Wouldst ruin thyself.'

'If I could ruin Ferrers,' said Bess passionately.

'That's not in thy power. The matter will not come to trial.' He went on. 'What concerns us chiefly now is what Ralph will do to punish thee.'

'When I leave here,' said Bess, 'I'll go live in Plymouth and see to my own life. It's not in his power to harm me.'

' 'Tis fully in his power,' said Hugh. 'Thou art his wife, taken in sin against holy wedlock. The Church might excommunicate thee.'

'I? When Ferrers has his children in every corner of the county. What of his sin?'

'Ah, Bess. For all thy wandering in the world, thou'rt innocent,' said Mary. 'Who can say which is Ralph's sin? Thine feeds at thy breast.'

'And more,' said Hugh. 'The church at Ancombe's in Ralph's gift. The priest's his man.'

'But I'm a citizen of Plymouth.'

'Thou'rt born, baptized and married in Ancombe, Bess. Thou helped to weave the web that traps thee.'

'But how may excommunication harm me?'

'Bess,' said Mary, shocked.

'It can harm thee,' said Hugh gravely. 'No excommunicant may trade or deal in business. There's further penalties.'

'I'll over-live them,' declared Bess. 'I'll herd cows for a living, break horses. I'll be a servant maid. I'll weave. And if that fail me, I'll tramp the roads like Ben Moore. The beadle's lash will warm me in winter.'

'Aye, if Ralph lets thee go.'

'Let me go? Why should he stay me? I've made him a joke in the parish. Sir Ralph the Cuckold.'

'Do not take him lightly, Bess.'

'Nay, forgive me, Mary, Hugh. I owe you much. I'm under your protection and he is your cousin.'

'We shall do our best for thee,' said Hugh.

Before a week had passed, Ferrers rode to Dauncey to demand that Bess come back to Ancombe. Bess refused to see him, but his shouted dispute with Hugh filled the house for an hour before he rode away.

'He says he'll bargain with you.'

'He's done that before.'

'He'll have you back, son and all. And his son by this village maid, too. Both will be acknowledged, but he will have you as his wife. You shall return.'

'Well, I'll not do it. The Church must give me separation.'

'How, Bess? Thy husband seeks to be reconciled.'

'Well, I'll not do it.'

Hugh looked troubled.

Next day Ferrers came again. This time there was no shouting. Ferrers spoke calmly to Hugh for some ten minutes, then rode away. Hugh said nothing to Bess, but his look of anxiety deepened. Bess wondered at this but her mind was taken up with the child. She was delighted to find that Judith's sister Dorcas, now a woman in her early thirties, was still in the Dauncey household. The two sat talking of old times. They spoke of Judith and Tom.

'So soon thou hast word of how they fare.'

'I go to the town each week and inquire,' said Dorcas.

The days passed. Christmas came and went, and then New Year. The boy's eyes began to take in the world round him, to recognize his mother's face with a tiny smile.

'We must consider how he may be baptized,' Bess told Mary. 'He shall be called Matthew.'

Mary looked at her, then burst out.

'Bess. Hugh will not tell thee. I must.'

'What is it Mary?' asked Bess in alarm.

Mary suddenly wept. 'Ralph has told Hugh that if we do not give thee up, he'll betray us.'

'How will he betray you?'

'Some years ago,' said Mary through her tears, 'Hugh gave shelter to a priest who fled the country. Ralph knows of this. We thought our secret safe with him, till now.'

'Why that is vile.'

'He'll do it though.'

'Mary, that was wrong of thee.' Hugh stood in the doorway.

'No, Hugh,' said Bess. 'She had full right to tell me. I'll not shelter at your cost. Nay – gainsay me not, Hugh. To-morrow send to thy cousin. Tell him I'll return, if he harms not my child.'

Hugh looked gratefully at Bess. ' 'Tis a heavy price to pay.'

'Not so heavy as you'd pay for holding me.'

In the morning, the message was sent to Ancombe and in the evening an answer came. Hugh came to Bess's room.

'I know not how to tell thee this, Bess. Ferrers gives his word the child shall not be harmed, on one condition.'

'What condition?'

'That in going home on Sunday morning, thou pass by Ancombe church and do penance for thy sin.'

'What?' said Bess, incredulous. 'Stand in a white sheet before the door, while the folk look on?'

'Aye, till time for prayers.'

'I'll not . . .' Bess checked herself. 'Nay, what does it matter. So long as he hurt not the child.'

'We will watch that, Bess,' said Hugh. 'I'll ride with thee to the church.'

Mary looked round, 'What, Dorcas? Dost listen at the door? What's that? Come here.'

But Dorcas, who had stood in the doorway, was gone.

At dawn on Sunday, Bess dressed herself. Another maid helped her, for Dorcas had not returned. She breakfasted with Mary, who looked sad and said little.

Bess mocked her gently: ''Tis not thou who must do penance, Mary. Ancombe is not the end of the world. I've travelled farther than that.'

Hugh came in, dressed and cloaked.

''Tis a fine, January morning, though cold, Bess. Art well-clothed?'

'Aye, and I shall have my white sheet to put over lest I shiver.'

'Hast thou all thou need, Bess?'

'Aye, I've my bundle with my Bible and sword. 'Tis fitting.'

'Thy child, how will he travel? Shall we have a nurse bring him?'

'Nay, young Matthew rides with me. I have a sling about my neck, and he'll sit snug inside. He must get used to horseback.'

'Farewell Mary. We'll meet soon.'

They walked outside. Bess mounted, took her child from Mary's hands and settled him in front of her. Hugh mounted, signalled to two of his men to follow, and they set off.

'Farewell Bess. God protect thee.'

'And thee.'

As they rode, the sun shone and the frost sparkled on the grass. Bess chatted calmly with Hugh, though beneath her speech, her thoughts ran more wildly. Somehow she must find a way to escape or endure.

'Courage, Bess,' she said to herself. 'Ben Moore fared worse and they could not put him down.'

Some two hours passed and the cottages of Ancombe came into view. People ran out and pointed. Dogs barked and children rushed into the street.

'They wait for thee by the church,' said Hugh.

The churchyard, under the small, squat tower, was crowded. Bess could see beyond the gate, where the priest, a man in grubby robes, stood with his attendants. Beyond him, nearer the church door, waited Ferrers, Susannah and their servants.

'Hugh, come no farther. I'll go on alone to the gate, and there put on my sheet and play my part before the people.'

She leaned over and took his hand. 'My thanks to thee, true friend, in spite of all that might divide us.'

'God send thee well, Bess. We are your friends for ever.'

He halted his horse. Bess rode on up to the churchyard. She turned and took from her saddle bag the white sheet that had been prepared with hastily cut arm and head holes. The crowd in the yard murmured and pointed.

'See, she has the child with her,' cried a woman.

'How bold my lady is,' said another.

The priest came forward down the path, waving his arms at the women to silence them. He stood in the gate and waited.

Bess slowly began to dismount, awkwardly because of the child she carried.

'Hold,' said a voice, nearby, almost at her elbow. 'Do not dismount, mistress.'

She looked down in surprise. A boy in a fisher's jerkin,

short and broad-chested, stood at her bridle.

'Wait. Stay on thy horse.'

'What's this, what's this?' called the priest, waddling forward.

'Nay, master priest,' called someone from among the crowd by the wall. 'The lady shall not be shamed in this manner.'

'Who speaks?' called Ferrers running with his men down the church path. Around the wall the crowd swirled and jostled.

A brown-clad figure mounted on the wall. He pointed at Ferrers.

'That cheapjack rogue did give his word to make the lady free. He broke it, cheated, lied, all to destroy her.'

'Stand down,' cried the priest. 'This is sacrilege.'

'Hold thy peace, blockhead, before we break thy popish altar-rail over thy addled head.'

A woman stepped from the crowd and stood between the priest and Bess.

'Judith!' called Bess.

Ferrers and his men tried to push forward. But from both sides of the wall sprang fishermen in woollen cap and canvas jacket, sticks in hand. Ferrers's sword was broken in his hand. His men, thrashed, ran for the church door, where Susannah Ferrers stood motionless, staring in silence at the riot.

'Now, Tom lad, lead the horse down to the ferry, and quickly,' called Judith.

Bess turned the horse, and with young Tom at the bridle, set off on the road away from the church. Around them streamed fishermen and weaver women forming a solid crowd about her, singing as they marched. And at the head of the crowd ran Martin Fletcher, thin, weather-beaten, and elated.

At the Cattewater shore, boats were waiting. Some dozen of the crowd, Judith, Martin, young Tom and others, helped Bess and her child on board and followed her. The rest, waving and shouting, marched on towards the town, still singing. The boats pulled out across the water.

'Didst think we would forsake thee, Bess Morten?' said Judith.

Bess could not speak.

Martin leaned across the boat and touched the baby's cheek.

'Bess. Our ship lies in harbour, waiting to sail. If you will, we'll set thee ashore to go where fancy leads. Or if it pleases thee, we'll sail for Providence Point. We've a minister there, to batize thy child, and what is more . . .'

'You've berries and shellfish, too, I trow.'

'Enough for all. Wilt come, Bess?'

'I will. To voyage abroad has ever been my fancy.'

The boats came alongside the ship at anchor.

'Lead the way, Bess,' said Judith.

Others helped Bess climb the ladder to the ship's deck. And as she stepped down, a man, broad-shouldered, hair greying, came forward from the after deck. He took off his cap.

'What's thy pleasure, lady? Across the bay to Cawsand, and back for thy supper?'

'Nay, Tom,' cried Bess. 'To the world's end.'